CAST DOWN WORLD

By

James A. Haddock III

Copywrite © 2020

WEBSITE:

Jameshaddock.us
Haddockpublishing.com

CAST DOWN WORLD SYNOPSIS

In the summer of 2257, the asteroid Wormwood was closing in to strike Earth a glancing blow. Even a glancing blow would be catastrophic. Earth's governments and militaries united to try to shift Wormwood's path. Earth launched every nuclear missile she had and succeeded in changing its path, just enough to miss her surface. In doing so, shards from the asteroid, caused by the nuclear blasts, struck the earth. In those shards were spores that caused a change in all forms of life. Wormwood also changed Earth's magnetic field, affecting weather patterns and causing earthquakes and tidal waves.

The devastation caused society's collapse. Only the strongest survived the Great Dying. In the years that followed, mutations began to appear in animals and people. It was a time of lawlessness, where the only law was the one you could enforce. Cities and larger towns became walled city-forts. Some chose to live outside the city-forts as ranchers, farmers, and scavengers. They enforced the law with violence, and the law of the old west returned. Out of this came the Peacekeepers, modeled after the legendary Texas Rangers. They were empowered by the city-forts to be judge, jury, and executioner. They were a group of hard men: hated, feared, and respected.

This is the story of Price—a human mutation, raised in the frontier wilderness—who becomes a PK Scout.

CHAPTER 1

Darkness...

Nausea...

Something running in my eye...

Rain, cold rain...

Pain...

Flashes of lighting...

"Get up boy!"

I looked up, and there stood the old man in the rain. "Grandpa? You're dead, Grandpa. It's raining, Grandpa..."

The old man chuckled. "I know it's raining, boy. This is a good lesson for you to learn. You may need it someday."

"The only thing I'm learning is it's wet and cold."

"That's what I want you to learn. If you get wet and cold, and stay that way, you'll get colder. If you don't get warm and dry, you could die. And if you keep lying there, you are going to die. Get up, boy!"

I opened my eyes and lifted my head. "I gotta get up. If I stay here, I die. Get up, boy. You heard the old man," I said, smiling.

I pushed myself up into a sitting position and felt my head. A bullet had creased my head above my eye. The shooter must have been a good way off because I never felt his presence.

I cast my mind around for my horse but didn't see or feel anything. Rain was still coming down hard. That was good. It cut down on how far the shooter could see. Now I needed to get into the brush before the rain let up. There was no need to give the shooter a second shot at me.

I got to my feet unsteadily, stumbled across the road into the brush, and pulled my scout's cape hood up over my head. Once I was a few yards undercover, I stopped. I took some deep breaths to calm and center myself, and then checked my gear. My daypack was still on my back; the pistols were in their holsters, and my rifle was in my saddle scabbard.

Other than the crease on my head, I seemed to be all right. "Thank God for my hard head," I laughed to myself.

The question now is: Do I go after the shooter or find shelter? I guess I can find him, or them, another day. Head wounds are tricky things; no need to push my luck. Shelter first, and I'll find him later.

The storm was getting worse. Shelter would be nice, but there was little chance of that. I was fifty miles from the nearest ranch and sixty miles to the nearest City-Fort. This whole area was wilderness forest, but maybe I could find something. I headed northeast straight through the forest toward the City-Fort.

I moved through the woods, casting my mind and eyes about. The only other minds I touched were that of small animals, squirrels, mice, coons, and such. It was still raining, though not as hard. Lightning was still active, but it was finally easing off.

I stopped every hour or so for a few minutes. The bleeding from my wound had stopped, but I was no longer cold...just wet. If I was stationary for too long, I would get cold again. I'd have to keep moving until I found shelter or was able to build a fire. I was still too close to the ambush site for a fire, so I moved on.

It was after midnight when I felt it. I froze in place. My mind had touched another mind—two minds actually, a horse and rider. They didn't seem to be moving. The rider was unconscious and seemed to be hurt. I started easing toward them, taking my time. I sent calming thoughts to the horse as I drew closer.

I found them on a game trail. The horse was eating grass, and the rider was on the ground with his foot hung in the stirrup. As I stepped into the open, the horse looked at me but didn't move. I walked over and patted him.

"Good boy, good job."

The reins had been looped over the saddle horn. I loosened them and dropped them to the ground. The horse would stay in place now.

I eased the rider's foot out of the stirrup and gently lowered his leg to the ground. His leg didn't seem to be broken, but that knee would never be the same. He was still alive but was shot through the chest—through and through. The shooter must have been using armor piercing rounds, as the bullet went through his Peacekeeper's armor-plated vest.

If the PK lived, someone was going to die for this. If you shoot a PK and don't kill him, you might as well go ahead and shoot yourself and save the long run. They would find you no matter what or how long it took, and you were a dead man.

Lightning flashed, and I noticed an odd shape out of the corner of my eye. The next flash showed part of a roofline not far off the path. Just in case someone came by looking to finish what they'd started, we needed to move.

I picked up the PK and told the horse to follow me. He did. The PK was no lightweight. He weighed about 220 and was over six feet tall. I had no trouble handling the weight though. I was stronger than the norms, or normal men—quicker too.

The roofline I'd seen turned out to be a broken-down old barn, or what was left of it. Three walls and the roof were mostly still there. It was better than nothing. The dirt floor was dry, and the water flowed away from the foundation. I laid the PK down and gathered the makings for a fire. There was dry wood under the roof, so I got the fire started, unsaddled his horse, and laid his rifle and saddlebags out beside him.

I looked through his gear and got a pot out. I filled it with runoff water from the roof and put it on to boil. As I opened his vest to see how bad his wound was, I noticed the rank on his vest.

This was no everyday Peacekeeper, if there was such a thing. He was a PK Captain. The bullet had missed his lung, hitting him high in the left shoulder. He had put something in it to stop the bleeding, but was still in bad shape.

I got him out of his vest and wet clothes and began cleaning the wound with the hot water. Once that was done, I applied my anti-bac cream and a poultice from my daypack.

I cast my mind around and called up a few rabbits. I put them to sleep and harvested them for rabbit soup. While I waited for the soup to finish, I changed out of my wet clothes, cleaned my wound, and wiped down our weapons and gear.

I kept my eyes, ears, and mind open, but no one else was around at the moment. I refused to be surprised again. We were in a side room, so the fire was not visible from the outside. You can never be too careful. My aching head was a reminder of that.

My back was to the fire facing the door, as I drank the hot rabbit soup. I knew the PK was awake before he said anything. I waited.

"How long have I been out?" he asked.

I answered without turning. "Don't know. I found you about two hours ago." I got up and stepped over to him. "It's about 2:00am, if that helps any."

He nodded his head. "How bad?"

"The shoulder you know about, through and through. The knee was twisted pretty badly. You fell out of the saddle, foot hung in the stirrup." He nodded and glanced at his pistol and rifle. "I cleaned and reloaded you weapons. Round's chambered and ready to fire."

"You try on my vest to see if it would fit?"

"No, sir, that would be rude. I would at least wait until you died," I said, smiling. He chuckled, and I handed him a cup of hot soup.

"Thanks. The name's Vance, PK Captain Vance."

"They call me Price," I answered.

"My horse?"

"Outside the door there. Under cover, dry, and brushed down."

He nodded, "Obliged." I refilled his cup with hot soup and handed it back to him. He glanced at my head wound: "You look like you had some excitement too."

"Yeah, just before sundown. One second I was riding along, and the next I'm eating mud. Lost my horse and decided to make myself scarce. My plan was to make sure my head was ok. I'll eventually find my horse and track them later."

"You're a scout," he said, a statement not a question. I nodded. "Wise. Head wounds can be iffy."

"If you're feeling up to it, I'm gonna check your back trail to make sure we don't get any surprise guests."

"Yeah, I'm good," he answered.

"I'll be gone an hour or two, but if something happens and I don't make it back, we're about forty miles southwest of Stone Barn Ranch. You should be able to make it there."

He nodded, "Step lightly, Scout."

"You, too, Captain."

I made sure he had plenty of firewood and water close at hand before I left. My scout's cape was dry again and kept me mostly dry. Its muted browns, greens, and streaks of black blended nicely into the forest background, and my pants matched the cape. My grandpa said they used to call it something like a ghillie suit. Whatever a ghillie was.

I left the barn, moving out into the forest. Once in the forest, I stopped and centered myself. I took in the smells and sounds, becoming a part of the forest. I headed back down the trail, staying in the woods and brush to the side. I stopped at the path where I had found the captain. With this much rain, all signs of our passing would soon be gone. I cast about with my eyes, ears, and mind and moved on. It was still raining, so I could move a little faster and not have to worry too much about the sounds I made.

I had been moving about an hour and hadn't seen or felt anything. I was about to turn back when I felt a horse's mind, so I squatted down and waited. The horse didn't seem to be moving. I started making my way toward him, and as I did, I felt more minds. There were three men and four horses, and one of the horses was mine. I started sending calming thoughts to the horses. Inching closer to their camp, I could now hear them talking. They were in a foul mood.

"He's probably dead, or near to it."

"What makes you so sure?"

"Cause we ain't dead. If he was able, we'd be dodging lead right now."

"So you say. You said you shot two people, but we can't find either of them."

"Why don't you both shut-up and get some sleep. We'll move at first light. I'll take first watch and wake you in a few hours."

I waited for the two to go to sleep. I felt their minds slip into a deep sleep. I concentrated on them, one at a time, and put them into a deeper sleep.

The third one finally sat down and was still, so I did the same to him. Now all of them would sleep until I woke them. I learned how to make people deep-sleep by helping my mother. She was a healer, and I would put people to sleep when she had to do something painful. She told me not to let anyone know I could do it. She said it would make folks uncomfortable if they knew.

I searched the three and took all their weapons, no use taking chances. One of them had a top-shelf, armor-plated vest. Lucky for me, it was my size. I took it, and it fit nicely too.

It looked to be as good as Captain Vance's, just without the hole in it. He also had a nice derringer and a holdout gun. Sheathed in his gator was a nano-bladed long knife, an exceptional find. Nanos were incredibly sharp and could cut through most armor and bone without ever slowing down. I put it in my daypack. The horses were still saddled, so I tied the three over their horses, mounted mine, and led them back toward the barn where I had left the captain.

***

After getting all the horses under shelter, I stopped short of the side room in the barn and walked close to the opening. I didn't feel like getting shot twice in as many days.

"Captain Vance, don't shoot. It's me, Price."

"You alone?"

"No, but they are all tied across their saddles at the moment. No danger."

"Come ahead."

I kept my hands in plain sight as I stepped into the doorway. He had his gun on me. "Tied over their saddles? They dead?"

"No, they're just knocked out."

"How many?"

"Three. I found them about an hour down your back trail with my horse. I had to wait until they were asleep to take them."

He lowered his gun. "Can you bring them in here?"

"Sure." I carried each one in, setting them against the wall across from the captain.

"Price, in my saddle bags you'll find a data pad and handcuffs. Get them cuffed, and then we'll see whom we got. Although, I do recognize two of them."

I did as he asked. I used the data pad to take their fingerprints and pictures. Then I cuffed them and handed the data pad to him.

He nodded his head. "Yep, Leroy and Tommy Jefferson and Will Carlson. They're all wanted on multiple counts of murder, horse theft, arson, pretty much everything. There's a reward of five thousand dollars each, dead or alive. Not bad for a day's work, Price."

I smiled. "No foolin', fifteen thousand dollars. Yep, that is a good day's pay all right. Captain, if you're good for a bit, I'd like to see to the horses."

"Yeah, go ahead. I'll wait for these yahoos to wake up. Their gear belongs to you too. You brought them in, so you reap the rewards."

"In that case, I'll go check on my horses," I said, smiling.

The horses were good stock, though one was better than the others. He had a fine new saddle and a camo hard case strapped to his side. I opened it and found an AR-10 Sniper Rifle.

"Well, well, well, very nice, and thank you," I said, smiling, as all their equipment was now mine. I also found the AP rounds that had been used on the captain.

I wiped it clean and dry and put it back in its case. After

unsaddling the horses, I took care of them. I laid out all their gear, which was now my gear. Most of it was new and high in quality. I also found over six thousand dollars in one's saddlebags and more than a thousand in the others' saddlebags combined.

I sat back looking at my loot. I'd been scouting on my own for three years and had made a few finds, but nothing big. I had either made or bartered for most of my gear, so all of their stuff was better than mine. My scout's cape was the only thing I favored over my haul.

We scouts wasted nothing. When we found a dead man, we searched him and salvaged anything of value. I traded out my day-pack for a better one and most everything in it, with the exception of my mother's meds. I rearranged saddlebags, horses, guns, knives, clothes, pretty much everything, and packed the rest of the gear away. I put the almost nine thousand dollars in my money belt and went back to the fire.

"Captain, if all their gear belongs to me, that includes what they are wearing too, right?"

He smiled, "Yep."

I walked over to the three and checked their minds to make sure they were still out. The man I took the armored vest from was about my size. He was wearing new boots and Kevlar gators. I took them off of him and tried them on. They fit. I also took his new leather and Kevlar armored bracers. I already had all of their hats, so the only things I left on them were their pants and shirts.

I moved back over to the fire and started cleaning and checking my new guns. I strapped the nano knife in my new gator, just like the man had worn it. "Captain, you have enemies?" I asked.

"I would imagine. Most PKs do."

I nodded. "Anyone who would pay big money to see you dead?"

He looked at me. "Why do you ask?"

"Well, those three there," I chin pointed, "had almost all new gear and about nine thousand dollars in cash. Your sniper," I pointed with my chin again, "had an almost new AR-10 and AP rounds. He was holding the most cash—over six thousand dollars.

Seems someone don't like you and is willing to pay good money to have you done away with."

He looked at the sniper. "Well, ain't that a tale. That bears thinking on."

I didn't want the captain getting suspicious, so I started to wake the three up. I also put the suggestion in their minds that they had been hit in the head and had terrible headaches.

When they woke, they were not happy. They cursed, kicked, and were spitting mad. The captain let them wear themselves out before he said anything.

"You are all charged with multiple crimes. The latest being attempted murder and conspiracy to murder a Peacekeeper Captain, namely me. If found guilty, it carries an automatic death sentence. The evidence against you is substantial. However, the first one to tell me the name of the one who hired you, I'll not hang."

"We don't know nothing!" the younger brother shouted.

"Then you shall hang."

"Carlson hired us, but we don't know who hired him," the older brother said. Carlson wasn't saying anything.

Faster than you can say, "Don't do it," the captain shot both brothers in the head, killing them instantly. Will Carlson just sat there staring at the captain.

"Well, Mr. Carlson, it seems there will be no witness to you giving me the name I want."

He glanced over at the two dead men and shook his head.

"Not possible. I never saw his face clearly and don't know a name. He called himself Mr. Black, but I'm sure that was not his real name."

The captain nodded. "Where did you meet him?"

"City-Fort Austin about three months ago."

"He tell you why he wanted me dead, give you any details?"

"Not really. Twenty-five thousand dollars to kill you, half in advance. He did speak with a southern drawl though. But I think he was faking it, didn't sound quite natural."

"How did you know where I was headed to setup the ambush?"

"We didn't. This was the fourth time we had gotten ahead of you on the most likely trail you'd take, and we finally picked the right one."

"Why shoot the scout?"

"I assumed he was with you. I didn't want a scout on my back trail. The fact that I'm sitting here, and he's wearing my boots, proves my point."

I smiled.

The captain nodded. "Any last requests?"

"Yeah, give us a decent burial, don't leave us hanging for the crows."

"I'll take care of it," I said.

"Thanks, scout," he said. I nodded.

Those were his last words. I went outside. The rain had stopped, and I got busy digging three graves.

CHAPTER 2

That night, the fever hit the captain and rode him hard for three days. I did what I could with what little I had and what wild roots I could find to help him. I sent calming thoughts to him when the nightmares came, which kept him at peace. Mostly, I just kept him hydrated with clean water and rabbit soup. The fever finally broke, but it took him another week to regain enough strength to travel.

We'd talk around the fire at night.

"I've worked with some scouts over the years. Y'all don't seem to talk much," he said one evening.

I smiled. "Not much," I answered. He smiled. "It's a habit we're taught. Less talk is better. Sound travels and so does information. Less talk stops both. Most people don't want to talk to us anyway. We make most folks uncomfortable. They say we're strange, not all human." I chuckled. "I'll admit we don't do anything to stop the rumors. It halts a lot of questions. Truth is we are just like everyone else. Some of us are empaths and can sense feelings in others. A few have a stronger gift, but they don't like to be around crowds. They say it's too loud in their heads."

"You have the gift?" he asked.

I shrugged. "Minor. It makes me good with horses and small animals."

That was the answer mom taught me to give. If anyone knew how strong of an empath and telepath I was, I would be thought a freak or worse. I was taught to shield my mind and hide my gifts. Not even other clan members knew how strong my gifts were.

"You married, Cap?" I changed the directions of the conversation.

"Nah, come close a few times, but the job got in the way.

You?"

"No. Too young, I haven't earned my place or proved my worth yet."

"If anyone asks me, I'd say you had. Most people would have left me where I lay or killed me for my gear and horse."

"I'd never leave a man the way I found you. Bad karma, what goes around comes around. There may come a day when someone finds me like I found you. I'll be wanting them to help me like I helped you. My grandpa said that's what folks did back in the 'before days.' Said folks helped each other. Said if those days were to return, that was a good place to start. Folks helping folks."

"Your grandpa sounds like a fine man."

"He was," and I said no more. I rolled up in my blanket and let sleep take me. I didn't dream much, but when I did, they were vivid.

***

Chores and school homework were done, and I was practicing my fighting moves. Dad called them 'katas.' I thought it looked more like dancing.

I knew Mom and Grandpa were watching me from inside the house. They were talking about me. I continued my kata, and Grandpa came outside and watched me.

He came over and joined me; it really did look like dancing. We kept moving as we talked.

"Your Dad been working with you?"

"No, sir."

"Who has?"

"No one. I watch you and Dad and do what you do. I can remember everything I see."

"You're doing well."

"I can do even better. I just need more practice."

"You're right. You'll get better if you keep practicing."

"I watch when they spar too. I look for places I can do better —weaknesses in their fighting style—so I can be better."

"Good, that's how you improve. I was talking to your mom. She's worried about you."

"I know. I can feel her worry."

He nodded. "Do you know why she's worried?"

"No, sir."

"It's because you don't talk much and don't have many friends. Is it because you can feel them too?"

"Yes, sir. They think I'm strange."

"You're not strange; you're different. Does your head hurt when you are around people, or when you feel their emotions or thoughts?"

"Only around certain people, not everyone."

"We'll work on that. I can teach you how to close your mind, like closing a door. Let's practice some punches and kicks."

"Yes, sir."

Grandpa started working with me in the evenings, helping me improve my fighting skills. Mom also started working with me, teaching me about herbs, plants, and medical skills. She also helped me with mind training. They both said I was a natural, and I improved quickly.

"Grandpa, Dad's been gone a long time."

He looked at me, "He has," and he went back to working the leather. "The frontier is a dangerous place, son. You never know when the expedition you're on will be your last. That's why we train so hard. The world is a hard place, and she has no sympathy. Remember that."

It was two years before I accepted that my dad was probably not coming home. I intensified my training, vowing I would do my best to always return from expeditions.

***

I looked up to see what the laughter was about. Mandy lay sprawled on the path. Someone had tripped her, and I knew that someone was Chuck. He was always doing that sort of thing. Chuck was big for his age and was a good fighter. Those two things combined to turn him into a bully. I didn't like him, and there was no love lost because he didn't like me either.

"Can't walk either, mute girl. What else is wrong with you?" His gang laughed.

I pushed past the circle and helped Mandy up. "Chuck, you know her name is Mandy."

Mandy signed to me, °Thank you.°

I signed back. °You're welcome.°

"I'm sorry, Price, I didn't know she was yours."

"Why don't you grow up?" I said, turning back to Mandy.

"You going to make me?"

I knew the punch was coming before he threw it. I ducked under it and put my foot out. He had put his whole body into the punch. He flew past me, tripped over my foot, and fell face first into the dirt.

Everyone laughed. He came up in a killing rage and attacked me. Everyone scattered. He was six inches taller than me and outweighed me by fifty pounds. His blind rage made defeating his attacks easier. I could tell he was not going to stop until he killed me, so I needed to end this.

He saw the opening I offered, and he took it. I slipped under his punch and elbow struck his chin. He went down...out cold. Everyone was staring at me open mouthed. No one had ever done that to Chuck. Mandy grabbed my hand and led me away.

When we got to Mandy's house, her mother came out on the porch. Mandy feverishly hand signed to her.

Her mother looked at me. "Mandy says you fought Charles."

"Yes, ma'am."

"Why?"

"He tripped Mandy and didn't like being called on it. He swung first."

"You knocked him out?"

"He wouldn't stop, so I had to before someone got hurt."

"Thank you for bringing her home."

"Yes, ma'am. How did you learn to sign?"

"We have books we learned from."

"May I borrow one?" Mandy was grinning from ear to ear.

"You may."

Chuck never was much of a bully after that day, but I always kept an eye on him just in case.

***

Captain Vance was getting better. I had scouted the area and found a few old houses and cars, rusted heaps mostly. I also found what was left of a blacktop road that cut through the forest. Nothing of value. We did get deer for a change from rabbit.

"You still planning on leaving in the morning, Captain?"

"Lord willing."

"Where we headed?"

"City-Fort Tulsa to get you paid."

"I like the way you think, Captain," I said, smiling.

We took it slow the first few days, following the blacktop. I kept my mind open for other minds that might prove to be a problem.

"Price, what are your plans after Tulsa?"

I shrugged. "Back to scouting the frontier, it's what we do."

"Would you consider scouting for the Peacekeepers?"

"What's it pay, and what's the duty?"

"PK Privates make thirty dollars a month plus room and board. Scouts operate a little different. They don't work all the time, only when we call on them. While they are working, PK Scouts make fifty dollars a month plus room and board. They also keep a quarter of anything they find and map. I owe you my life twice over, so I'll bring you on as a PK Scout Sargent. You'll make one hundred dollars a month, have room and board, and half of anything you find and map. It may help you during lean times. If you run across bad men, you can choose to activate yourself, take care of business, and charge the City-Fort for your time."

"Which City-Fort?"

"Any of them. That's part of the Peacekeeper Charter. When you identify yourself as a Peacekeeper, they must feed, house, and resupply you."

"What's the downside?"

He smiled. "Any Peacekeeper can request your help, and you have to help them. Any City-Fort can request you, and you have to help. On the bright side, once you get twenty years of active service, you will get a monthly check of fifty percent of your retirement rank pay for the rest of your life. Well, if you live that long," he laughed.

I laughed. "You paint such a rosy picture."

"You think on it."

"Uh-huh. What about reward money on outlaws, do I get that?"

"Half, but if you are working with another PK, you split it with him."

"Better than nothing, I guess. What about training?"

"The first part takes a week. Then you would ride and work with a PK, but you've already done that part," he said, smiling. I nodded and returned his smile.

Late afternoon, we started looking for a campsite. We were in no hurry, so we planned to stop earlier than we normally would. We spotted an open area on a rise a short distance away and headed for it.

As we arrived, I felt the presence of another mind. It was in anguish and pain. "You stay here, Cap, I'm going to scout around a bit."

"Okay, I'll start setting up camp."

I moved off toward the mind I was feeling. It felt like a horse's, or a dog, but not really. I began sending calming thoughts. To my surprise, I received back a plea for help, not in words but feelings.

I kept moving toward the call for help and entered into a clear area spotted with tar pits. In one of the tar pits was a large horse, but not a horse.

"Oh, my Lord, a Talon Foot!"

I moved around the clearing to get to her. She was stuck fast and had worn herself into exhaustion trying to free herself, which only made her sink deeper.

I approached her. "Easy girl, stop fighting, I'll get you out."

You help? Another surprise. She sent me thoughts in words.

Yes, I help. Stay calm and don't move.

She lay there breathing hard, looking at me. I sent her thoughts of what I was going to do and what she should do to help me help her.

I shook my lasso out and threw the loop over her head. I looped the rope around my saddle horn and had my horse start backing away, putting tension on the rope.

She reached out with her taloned forefeet and started pulling herself forward. Luckily, the pit was not deep, and we got her out relatively easy. Once she was free, she lay there for a while and rested. She was shaking from adrenaline and exhaustion.

I dismounted and approached her slowly. I thought to her that I was going to take the lasso off. She lowered her head to me, and I removed it.

Are you hurt? I sent images of a hurt leg.

No, tired only.

I'll stay with you until you have rested. You would be an easy meal for wolves or a bear.

Not so easy.

I smiled. *No, not so easy. May I check your rear hoofs, maybe clean them out?*

She looked at me, sending gratitude.

I broke some pine branches and wiped her hooves off, looking them over. They seemed ok.

You should be fine, just sore from your struggling. Again, I felt her gratitude.

After a half hour, she was on her feet, unsteadily, but up. She stood over eighteen hands tall. She walked over to a puddle of water and drank deeply. While she drank, I got more pine limbs and cleaned her off as well as I could.

Most of that is going to have to wear off.

She blew, and I felt frustration. *Foolish as a colt.*

I smiled. *We all are sometimes.* I felt her agreement. *Where is *your herd?**

They left when I fell in black mud. I am dead to them.* I felt sorrow from her.

I mounted my horse and started back to camp, and she fell in right behind me.

You are free to go where you will.*

I go with your herd.* I felt finality in the thoughts, so I didn't argue. I'd let her do as she wanted.

On the way back to camp, she stopped and wallowed in the mud, covering all the tar. As I rode into camp, Cap was staring at us.

"What in the world is that?"

"We call them Talon Foot horses; they're very rare. I found her stuck in a tar pit, and she followed me home."

He chuckled, "I told my Ma a similar story about a dog one time."

I smiled, unsaddled the horses, and brushed them down. Talon lined up for her turn, just like the other horses. So I treated her just like one of them. I felt contentment from her. I couldn't do much other than brush her mud and tar-covered body, but I did what I could.

We sat at the fire eating. "You going to ride her?"

I laughed. "Not likely. You don't break a Talon Foot to ride. You befriend them, then maybe, just maybe, they will allow you to ride them."

The next morning, after a breakfast of hot jerky broth, we got ready to leave. I started to saddle my horse, and Talon shouldered her way past my horse.

You ride me now. I am much better. You are mine.*

She showed her carnivore teeth and growled at the other horses. There was no further argument from any of us.

I started to put the halter on her.

Nothing in mouth.*

I took the bit off the bridle, and she let me put it on her. I really didn't need one anyway. She felt where I wanted to go and took me there. She was a wonderful ride, and we moved as one.

Cap just shook his head.

The other one is not like you. I cannot hear him, and he cannot hear me.

No, we are not the same. I can feel and speak to some animals and some people. He cannot.

***

We arrived in City-Fort Tulsa the next day. Cap accompanied me to the Provost office where I collected the rewards, and then we walked across the street to the Goldman Bank office. I already had an account with them, not that there was much in it. They had offices in every City-Fort. I deposited twenty thousand dollars and kept the rest in cash.

"What have you decided about becoming a PK Scout?"

"When would I have to do the training you talked about?"

"In a few days. It would take a week to complete."

"Okay, I'll do it. I need to stable my horses."

"Peacekeepers have their own stable here, and it won't cost you anything."

We made our way to the PK livery. Talon was getting a lot of attention.

The Stable Master looked at Talon. "She yours?" That was a stupid question.

"Nope, I'm hers," I said, smiling. "Just show me her stall, and I'll come every day to care for her."

"Thank goodness." They took care of the rest of my horses.

"Scouts usually stay at the livery," Captain Vance said. "They want to be close to their horses. I'll show you to your room." He showed me my room, and then handed me a PK Scout Sargent badge. "Show this any place that serves food, and they will feed you along with two beers, or whatever you're drinking. Check in with me tomorrow, and we'll get paperwork done and set you up to start training."

I nodded. "Sounds good, I'll see you tomorrow."

After the captain left, I put my gear and supplies in my room and went to find something to eat. I went back to an inn we had passed. They were probably used to seeing Peacekeepers in there, so I should have no trouble getting fed.

I took a table along the wall out of the way, and a serving girl came over. "What'll you have?"

I showed her my badge. "What do you recommend?"

"Beef stew's fresh and so is the bread," she answered.

"And a beer." I said. She nodded and turned away.

In a few short minutes, she returned with my order. It was good, and I ate slowly, observing the people around the room.

Everyone was quiet and minded their own business. Just the way I liked it, quiet meal and to be left alone. When I finished, the serving girl brought my bill and a second beer. I signed it and sat with my own thoughts as I enjoyed my beer.

On the way back to the livery, I stopped at the trading post. I was greeted by one of the clerks. "How can I help you, sir?"

"I need some clothes." I was dressed in my trail clothes and I wanted some town clothes. Because of the reward money, I could now afford them.

"Right over here, sir."

I picked out a couple shirts—one green and one grey—and grey-black pants that matched the vest and coat. I needed socks and underwear. Mine were in sad shape. I had always admired those Stetson hats, so I bought me one that matched the coat and a belt.

"There is a changing room over there where you can try them on, sir."

I nodded and went over to the changing room. I was very careful about people seeing me without my clothes on. They would think me deformed if they saw my bony scales. The scales covered my joints, forearms, shins, knuckles, spine, and neck. They were the same color as my skin and bone hard. They had saved me a lot of pain and wounds in fights I'd had.

The clothes fit fine, and I look good in them, if I do say so myself. I changed back into my trail clothes, told the clerk to wrap them up, and I'd take them.

"What have you got that will remove tar?"

He thought a moment. "Turpentine, maybe?"

"I'll try it. Give me a gallon and a bundle of rags." I paid the man and thanked him for his help.

I took my purchases back to the livery and put my new clothes in the room. After gathering the rags and turpentine, I took Talon outside.

"Let's try to get you cleaned up."

I soaked a rag in the turpentine and started scrubbing Talon. It was working.

Stinks.

Yeah, but it's getting you clean.

It took me the rest of the afternoon, but she was finally free of the tar. I washed her with soap to get the turpentine off of her.

Feel better.

Good, you look better too.

I took my time brushing her out. She was enjoying the attention.

After I finished, I put her back in her stall and went to get cleaned up myself. I took a bath, shined my boots, and put on my new clothes. I left most of my weapons in the room and went looking for a barber. I found one down the street and went in. There was only one man ahead of me, so in no time, I had a shave, a haircut, and was on my way to Ruth's restaurant. According to the barber, it was the best steak house in City-Fort Tulsa.

Ruth's was a big place and busy. When I went in, I found Ruth herself seating guests. She took one look at me. "Peacekeeper?"

"Yes, ma'am."

"Come on in, hon', let's get you fed."

She sat me out of the way, but where I could see the door and most of the room. I never placed an order, but a plate with the biggest steak I'd ever seen sat there, sizzling hot off the grill, with a side of fried potatoes and onions. Ruth sat hot coffee down. "You need anything else, hon', just yell."

"Yes, ma'am." She winked at me and was off again.

As soon as I finished my steak and potatoes, the dishes were cleared away and replaced with apple pie desert and fresh, hot coffee.

Miss Ruth stopped by. "How was everything?"

"Ma'am, that was the best meal I have ever had."

She smiled, "This your first time in?"

"Yes, ma'am, PK Scout Sargent Price, at your service."

She shook my hand. "Ruth Anderson. Pleased to meet you, Sargent."

"You stop in anytime you pass through; I love all my Peace-keepers. My son was a Peacekeeper Sargent, but we lost him a year ago."

"My condolences, Miss Ruth."

"Taking care of you boys helps. It makes me feel like he's still with me."

"We are honored that you feel that way, Miss Ruth. If there is ever anything I can do, please ask."

She smiled. "You step lightly, Scout, and come see me again."

They never brought a bill for me to sign, but I left a nice tip for the service. I called it a night and went back to my room.

CHAPTER 3

The next morning, I mucked out Talon's stall and made sure she had plenty of food and water. While I was brushing her down, the Stable Master walked up.

"You keeping all your horses?" he asked.

"No, I'm planning on selling three of them."

"The PK will buy them and pay you top dollar too. Which three are you selling?"

Keep him. Talon was looking at the big one I had been riding when I pulled her out of the tar pit. *He's the best of the four, and he'll follow me close.*

"The three on the end," I said, smiling.

"PK will pay you forty dollars apiece for them."

It was a fair price. "Done," I answered.

I also sold him three saddles and tack and traded one saddle for a packsaddle. I had never had enough gear to justify owning a packhorse, until now, and I planned to take advantage of it. I could now afford to enjoy the trail a little more without being wasteful.

I met Captain Vance at the PK office, signed my PK authorization paperwork, and was sworn in. The next ten days seemed to drag by. I'd take care of Talon, go to PK School, and eat lunch. Then I'd head back to PK School, take Talon out for some exercise, dinner, and finally off to bed. Mom used to call days like that groundhog days.

When I finished PK School, Captain Vance gave me a data-pad, which had all the current criminal wants and warrants on it. It also held the PK Law Library for my continuing study and reference. They had showed me how to use it in PK school.

"Which way you headed?" Captain Vance asked.

I thought a moment. "West, back out to the frontier."

"Keep in touch and step lightly, Scout."

"You too, Captain."

We shook hands and he walked away. He was a man of few words. I had a few things to do before I left Tulsa. I wanted to sell the extra gear I had and have a meal and beer.

I loaded the extra gear on the new packsaddle to see how the horse would handle it. I rode Talon, and the packhorse followed close behind without needing a lead rope. When we got to the trading post, there was a big Conestoga wagon with two yoke of Morgan oxen parked there. Those Morgan oxen were something; they were huge. They were oxen, but they were as big and powerful as Morgan horses.

Standing in front of the store, two men were in a heated discussion.

"That's robbery!"

"Look, Mister, I told you…I don't buy rigs like this."

"But you just offered to steal it from me."

"I offered to buy it from you. I'd have to resell it to make my money back. You don't have to sell it to me. You can take it somewhere else."

"What about all the equipment?" He pointed at things beside the wagon.

"The price was for everything. Take it or leave it, your choice." He turned and went back in the trading post.

I could feel the frustration, fear, and anger coming from the owner of the wagon. There was a woman and child standing to the side. They were also full of fear.

I dismounted and took the pack of extra gear off of the packhorse. "Morning, ma'am," I said as I passed her. She nodded. I went inside and walked over to an open trading table and sat the pack down.

"Good morning, sir."

He looked at the pack. "Trading or selling?"

"Selling."

He looked over everything and made his offer. It was a bit

low, but I felt he would go higher. I wanted information, so I took his offer. He paid me my money.

"What was all that outside?" I asked.

He harrumphed. "Darn fool came out here from back east somewhere and thought it was easy living and open land. He found out differently real quick. He's selling everything to either go back or find work inside the walls."

"Yep, it's a hard country no doubt," I said, thinking. "Good day to ya." And with that, I went back outside, stepped onto the porch, and looked toward the wagon. As the man and woman were reloading their goods, I had the beginning of an idea rolling around in my head.

You making our herd larger?

Maybe.

I walked to the back of the wagon where they were working. "Pardon the interruption."

"Yeah?" the man answered.

"I couldn't help but overhear your discussion with the trading post manager."

"Crook, more like."

"If you are determined to sell out, I might be interested in buying." He gave me a hard look. I could feel his anger starting to build, so I started talking before it blew. "I'm sure I'd give a better price on your things, as I'm not buying to resale. I'm buying to keep." I felt his anger die.

"Look, mister," he started. "I'll tell you straight. I got over four thousand dollars tied up in this, but it was worth it. We bought only the best—best stock, best wagon—only the best."

I nodded. "Can I have a look inside?"

"Help yourself."

I climbed up inside. There was furniture, a stove, tools, everything to set up a house. It was quality stuff, no doubt. I climbed down, and all three of them were looking at me.

"You planning on staying in Tulsa or going back east?" I felt his anger start, and I held up my hand. "The reason I ask is you may need some of your furniture and goods to set yourselves up here if you are staying."

His shoulders sagged. "To be honest, I don't know. Ain't much to go back to. I made big talk of how I was going to make it big out here." His wife put her hand on his shoulder.

"What did you do back east?"

"Carpenter, wagon and wheelwright."

"That so," I said, looking past him at an empty wagon station building with a fenced stockyard. "Did you build this wagon?"

"I did."

I nodded and climbed under the wagon to have a look. He had used one-ton truck axles, leaf springs, and shocks. He'd made wood and iron wheels. On one side was a solar-powered refrigerator and freezer that could hold a whole beef. It was quality craftsmanship to be sure. I got up and looked over the rest of the wagon and made my decision.

"As it happens, I'm looking to hire a carpenter, wagon and wheelwright to run my wagon station. I'd like you to repair and build wagons. After seeing these Morgans, I may bring some more in."

"Truly?" his wife asked.

"Yes, ma'am. Would you be interested in the job?"

"I would indeed, sir."

"You finish loading the wagon. I'll be back in an hour, and we'll talk more." We shook hands, and they got back to work.

I walked down the street toward the old wagon station. Once there, I went through the place. It needed some work, but it was solid. There was a blacksmith's shop next door, so I stepped over to see who owned the station.

When I walked in, the blacksmith called out, "Can I help you?"

"Yes, do you know who owns the wagon station?"

"That would be me," he answered.

"It for sale?"

"For the right price, it might be."

I felt his emotions right away. He was dying to get rid of the place. "What are you asking for it?"

He thought a moment. "One thousand dollars for the land, buildings, and everything in them."

"Ain't nothing in them. Sorry to have wasted your time." I turned to walk away.

"That's true! I did sell everything out of it. I'll take five hundred dollars."

I laughed, "I may be young, but I ain't that young. I'll give you seventy-five dollars."

He looked at the place and shook his head. "A hundred dollars."

"Done," I answered. I paid him, and he signed the papers over to me.

I walked back to the trading post. They had finished loading the wagon and were waiting for me.

"By the way," he said, "I didn't catch your name."

"Price," I answered, shaking his hands.

"Ben Oliver, my wife Nora, and little Ben."

"Pleased to meet you all. If you are ready, we can move down to the wagon station and continue our dealings."

I mounted Talon and led the way down to the wagon station. We went inside and looked around.

"This is not a working station?" Ben asked.

"Not yet, that's where you come in. I provide the capital; you provide the labor and management, and we split the profits. I'll pay for all the repairs and supplies you need to set the place right and get you started. You will also get a hundred dollars a month guaranteed. Once we start making more than that, you'll make a greater salary. I'll give you twenty-five hundred dollars right now for the oxen and wagon."

His wife elbowed him. He and I smiled. "We accept," he said as we both laughed. Nora's face turned red.

"Let's get a list of all we need to put this place right and get set up for business. Also, a list of all you need to start repairing and building wagons. We need to get over to the bank and set up a business account as well."

"That would be Nora's area of expertise. She is my accountant."

I nodded, "Fine with me. I guess the first thing we need to do is get the wagon unloaded and your house set up."

We unloaded the wagon and put their furniture in the house. It was separate from the station. I took Talon and my packhorse back to the PK stables and spent the night there.

After breakfast the next morning, I started buying supplies and had them delivered to the wagon station. We opened a bank account under the business name of, "Tulsa Wagon Station." It took us a week of work before we were satisfied and opened it for business.

"Ben, I want you to make some modifications to my wagon."

"Okay, what did you have in mind?"

"I want chuck wagon compartments added to the sides, not the back. I don't want the additions to hamper the loading and unloading of freight."

"No problem, I'll get right on it."

"Also, you can charge any additions made to the house or station to the business."

"Alright, Nora will keep a clear record of all costs."

"Sounds good."

I moved from the PK livery to the station's barn and made me a place to sleep up in the loft. There were six stalls down one side of the barn, which was where Talon and the packhorse went. The other side was for wagon repairs and building.

I was brushing Talon when I felt them approaching. There was a man and four dogs. I kept brushing Talon, but I turned so I could see them. He was not a large man, but what he lacked in size his dogs more than made up for. They must have weighed two hundred pounds apiece. He was dressed in plain frontier clothes, and they were in good repair.

"Greetings, brother." He spoke to me in clannish.

"Greetings, brother, come in and be welcome," I answered in clannish, stepping forward to shake his offered hand. His dogs stayed alert, two facing me, two facing the door.

"You'd be the PK Scout called Price?"

"I am."

"They call me Sheppard."

"What can I do for you, Sheppard?"

"That depends. Are you planning on staying in Tulsa or taking your wagon back out on the frontier."

"Back out on the frontier." He nodded his head.

"In that case, I'd like to hire on with you. I cook, take care of camp, and my dogs will guard us and our stock at night. I also call up maverick cattle as we travel, and we make them part of our herd. The dogs keep them herded up when needed. When we get to a place to sell them, I get one-third of the sales price. One-third goes to the wagon and the last third to you. You also pay me ten dollars a month salary and give room and board for me and the dogs."

I thought a moment. "You ever haul freight between settlements?"

"Some."

"You know what we'd need to buy to make a profit trading what we'd haul between settlements?"

"I do."

"Okay, Sheppard, we'll make a run and see how we work out. Come on and let me introduce you to Ben Oliver. He manages the station for me."

We walked over to my wagon where Ben was working.

"Ben, this is Sheppard. He'll be driving and working the wagon. Show him what we've done, and see if he needs anything else added. Sheppard, get me a list of supplies we'll need and a list of supplies we'll be trading."

As I walked away, they were deep in conversation about the wagon. Sheppard's dogs were lying by the wall watching everything, and I went back to brushing and tending to Talon.

Increasing our herd?

Seems so. We'll see how it works out.

It will be a good herd.

Sheppard came back a good while later with both lists I'd asked for. "What did you think of the wagon?"

"She'll do. Ben does good work. I asked for a few changes to the chuck area, and he liked them."

I looked over the list, it was pretty detailed and long. "You good with the weight of all of this?"

"She'll handle that and then some."

"Okay, we'll start placing orders in the morning. I stay up in the loft. There's room up there for you and your dogs."

He glanced at the loft and nodded. Then, he went up, and the dogs followed him.

I looked over the list again. It was mostly staple goods—salt, sugar, flour, coffee (lots of coffee), beans, salt pork, nails, rope, simple hand tools, and multiple calibers of ammo. I added more to the ammo list.

"Hey, Price," Sheppard called down.

"Yeah?" I answered, looking up toward the loft.

"You ever buy large amounts of goods for trade here in Tulsa?"

"Nope, have you?"

"Yeah, a few times. I know where the warehouses are to get us the best prices."

"Good, we'll do that in the morning." He nodded and went back to what he was doing. I walked up into the loft. "Shep?"

He looked up. "Yeah?"

I handed him twenty dollars. "Expenses," I said, and he nodded. "I'll be back after a while." He nodded again. *"A man of few words,"* I smiled.

I saddled Talon and took her and the packhorse over to the PK livery. "Sargent Price, I figured you'd be gone by now."

"Not yet. I bought a business, and I'm getting it up and running before I go."

"Do tell."

"I opened a wagon station down by the front gate."

"By the blacksmith's place?"

"That's the one."

"Good for you. What brings you by?"

"I want to buy back one of those saddles I sold you. I have a man working for me now and may need a saddle horse from time to time."

"Sure, go pick out the one you want, and you can pay me what I paid you for it."

I got the best of the bunch and paid him. I put the saddle on the horse and waved goodbye to the Stable Master as I left.

The next morning, Shep led me to the warehouses where we could buy bulk goods. "You want to dicker for our goods?"

"You have a good relationship with them?"

"Pretty good."

"You do it then."

We went inside, and Shep gave him the lists of what we wanted. The man read it over, asked a few questions, and they started dickering on the price. I sat down to watch the show.

The hand waving and lies went to flying. Been a while since I'd seen such a show. Finally, they shook on a price.

"I sure have missed you, Shep," the man said, laughing. "No one dickers like you do."

"I'm out of practice. I think you got the better of me this time." We scheduled the pickup for two days later and started back toward the station.

"I'll be back later. I need to make a few stops." I nodded, and he and the dogs split off from me.

The next morning, Ben pronounced the additions to the wagon were complete, and we started loading our gear into it. Shep oversaw wagon operations, so I left the placement of supplies to him.

"If there is anything else you need, as far as cooking equipment, tell me and I'll buy it."

"I think we have everything covered, but I plan on preparing a meal out of it tonight to check everything. I'll know more after that. Please invite the Olivers to dinner. He should see how his designs work firsthand."

Shep's cooking was a hit with everyone, and the wagon's design worked perfectly. He did find a few things he'd missed, but they were easily purchased.

The next morning, we had the wagon at the loading dock when the warehouse opened. Shep oversaw the loading and placement of our merchandise in the wagon, and I paid our bill. By midmorning, we were leaving City-Fort Tulsa. A lot had happened in the last month, and I was ready to be back out in the open.

CHAPTER 4

We travelled about six miles that afternoon, as we didn't want too push the stock to hard the first day on the trail. We also wanted to check the wagon to make sure it was handling the load. After the camp chores were done and we had eaten, we sat by the fire enjoying hot coffee. Using camp chairs was new to me, but we did have a wagon, so why not?

"If you can take some game on the trail every few days that will stretch our supplies," Shep said.

"I can do that," I answered.

Shep looked after the stock except for Talon; I took care of her. She loved the attention. The dogs guarded the camp at night, and nothing came close that they didn't let us know about. I suspected Shep had a strong talent and knew as well as I did when anything approached our camp. How else was he planning to call up mavericks?

After a quick breakfast of bacon biscuits and coffee, we were off again early the next morning. We stopped at noon to butcher a deer I killed and had meat and bean burritos for lunch. However, we didn't want to stay where we butchered; predators would follow the smell of our kill.

We were five days out of Tulsa when Shep started gathering cattle. The dogs scouted the countryside for them, and if there were only one or two, they would drive them back to the wagon. If there were more, Shep rode out to them. He calmed them and checked for brands. If they had a brand, he'd send them home. Otherwise, he made them part of our herd. It was so simple. I don't know why I had never thought of it.

It wasn't long before we had 25 head of cattle, which made my job harder. I had to scout for water for our growing herd. The cattle stayed with the wagon, where Shep and the dogs protected them. When the wagon moved, they moved. We were doing well on water so far, and we found good water every few days. We weren't in a hurry to get anywhere, so the cattle gained weight nicely as time went by.

One or two of the dogs also started ranging out with me. I guess even dogs get bored walking around cattle all the time. Part of my duties as a PK Scout was to update maps in my data-pad. Every time I checked into a PK office it updated the central data post and downloaded any new info to mine. I had added a few places we found water that were not shown on the map.

We would usually let the cattle water at a watering hole, and then move off to set up camp. Other animals used the watering hole, including predators, but our moving cut down on confrontations. At night after supper, Shep would play his guitar and sing softly to the cattle. They would all come closer and lay down to listen to him play. They typically stayed that way until the next morning. It was one of the strangest sights I've ever seen.

Breakfast was bread and meat, left over from supper, and hot coffee. My mind tingled, "Four riders coming in, and I don't think it's for the coffee."

I could tell by the feel of their minds that they were up to no good. Shep got in the wagon with his rifle, and the dogs vanished into the brush.

I moved up to the front of the wagon, still holding my coffee. They reined up in front of me, looking around.

"Morning," I said.

"Morning," one replied.

"What can I do for you boys?"

"We think you got some of our cattle, and if you have, we are going to take them back."

"I see. What brand are you looking for?" That caught him off guard and he had no ready answer. "I think you're herd cutters, which is just a nice name for cattle thieves."

They went for their guns, and I sent their horses a thought of intense pain under their saddles. All four of them started bucking to get away from the pain. As the riders hit the ground, the dogs attacked. I took away the pain from the horses and got them calmed down. The riders were all dead. The dogs had ripped their throats out.

We stripped the bodies of anything useful: a few dollars, guns, and ammo. We did the same with their horses and added them to our herd. I took their pictures and fingerprints on my data-pad and hung the four in the trees beside the road with a sign that read, "Cattle Thieves".

"Shep, let's stay here another day. I want to back track their trail and see if they were up to anything else."

He nodded, "I'll be here."

Talon and I struck out following their back trail. It wasn't hard, as they weren't trying to hide anything.

A few miles further down the road, we came to a small ranch house and barn. The front door was open. A body was on the porch, and another by the barn. The only life I felt was the stock.

I dismounted and checked inside the house. It had been ransacked. There were three more bodies inside, a woman and two boys. The body at the barn appeared to have been a ranch hand. Inside was a wagon full of looted supplies. I found a shovel to dig the graves, but Talon had already started digging. Her big talons making short work of it. I wrapped the bodies in bed linen and laid them to rest all together.

There was a herd of two hundred cattle, of mixed brands, in the pasture behind the house. The brand on the barn door was, "BDN". The rest must have been what the cattle thieves brought in. I road through the herd, found all those with a non-BDN brand, and put it in their minds to go home to be fed. They started trotting off, and I was still left with about a hundred head of cattle and ten horses.

I sent a suggestion for them to stay together for safety. I took two of the horses back to the barn, hitched them up to the wagon, and looked around the barn for anything to salvage. There was a portable blacksmith's forge and small anvil, which I loaded into the wagon. After gathering the other items of value, I went back into the house. These folks didn't have a lot, as it was a small working ranch. They made a living but not much else. I took the food and left most everything there for someone else to salvage.

When I was ready, I sent to the cattle and horses that they were not safe unless they stayed with my herd. We started moving back toward where Shep was camped and arrived by late afternoon.

Shep took charge of the new herd and joined the two herds together. I unhitched the horses from the wagon and set them loose in the herd. Shep came up to the wagon as I was looking over the salvage, and I told him what I had found.

"Lazy trash, worse than animals. At least animals don't kill without reason. Greed ain't no reason."

"Look through this stuff. If there's anything you want to cross load or rearrange, we'll do it now and move out in the morning."

"Yeah, I see a few things, in case it rains. We'll put a tarp over it too."

We got to work. After supper, I got my data-pad out and wrote a report on the day's events. It would upload the next time I checked in.

Early the next morning, we were back on the road, following the road west. We moved a little slower with the bigger herd, but once we got them moving, we made good time. We no longer actively sought mavericks. But even so, the dogs kept bringing them in, and they'd stay with our herd. We stopped at small towns as we came to them, but we'd stay outside their walls.

We sold some supplies, equipment, and some beef along and along. We traded for fresh eggs, milk, and vegetables as we went. One rancher bought sixty head of our cattle at ten dollars apiece. He was trying to build up his herd and took mostly BDN stock. We gave him a bill of sale for the cattle.

When we met travelers heading east, we'd exchange information on trail conditions and sometimes do some trading. We did a good trade with the bigger ranches, resupplying them. They usually bought some cattle from us.

When we reached Oklahoma City-Fort, we sold the rest of our cattle and the extra horses. We traded the extra wagon, horse tack, and all the stuff we salvaged from the cattle thieves and ranch. We then paid the difference in cash for our resupply. And in case the need for emergency repairs came up while on the trail, we kept the portable forge and anvil.

While Shep saw to the supplies being loaded, I went to the PK Office and updated my data-pad. I talked with a PK Sargent about conditions west of OCF. He said it was quiet, as far as he knew. I filled him in on conditions east of OCF.

We decided to stay a few days in OCF to rest the Morgans and ourselves. We rented a fenced lot inside the wall close to the gate. One of us and two of the dogs were always with the wagon and stock. We had made good money on our cattle and trade. Shep and I worked well together, so we decided to continue with our arrangement.

After supper that evening, we made coffee at our wagons.

"We still pulling out in the morning?" Shep asked.

"Unless you know of a reason not to. If those wheels ain't turnin', we ain't earnin'."

"That's a fact. No, no reason I can think of not to move on."

"You ever been to Amarillo, Shep?"

He nodded. "Years back. Be a good place to head to do some trading. Lots of cattle country between here and there too. We'll need to head south to the Red River and follow it to keep the cattle watered though."

"Yeah, water will be the thing we'll need most out there. South to the Red it is."

We pulled out early the next morning. We made ten miles a day for the first two days, and then we started rounding up mavericks. On the third day, Shep put the dogs to work. After that, we averaged four to five miles a day as we moved. Again, we took our time so the cattle could put weight on.

The more time I spent with Talon, the closer our minds became. She learned from me and I from her. My mind became more focused, and my talent was growing stronger.

I could now sense minds at a greater distance and exert more of my will over them. I even started to practice killing with my mind; it would save on ammo. I had been able to kill rabbits at close range, but now I could kill at greater distances. I started with small animals, and then worked my way up to deer, boar, and finally a cow. We ate everything I killed, and it did save ammo. I kept my growing talent to myself. There are some habits you don't want to get out of.

When we crossed to the Red, we had thirty-five head of cattle and two horses in our herd. We fell back into our old patterns, moving slowly all day, except when I made a kill. At night, Shep sang the cattle into a calming rest.

We moved northwest along the Red, gathering mavericks and trading when given the opportunity. Shep had been right; there were a lot of mavericks out on the open frontier. We only kept the mavericks, sending anything with a brand back home.

There were small abandoned towns that dotted our route, but they had long ago been stripped clean of any salvage. If the town was close enough, I would sometimes ride through just out of curiosity. There wasn't much to this one.

I smell smoke. Talon turned toward the smell. *Large predator smell too.*

She flashed a vision of a grizzhorn. They were bad news. They were mutated grizzly bears with forward facing horns like a bull. And they were mean, mean as a, well, a grizzhorn. I pulled my rifle from its scabbard, as we moved slowly toward the smell of smoke.

As we drew nearer, my mind started to get the tingle of another mind. It was full of anger and pain. I could tell it was close, but I couldn't tell how close. I did not like being on this narrow street. We were closed in.

I felt Talon's muscles bunch an instant before she jumped. The grizzhorn roared, as it exploded from a storefront. Its huge, clawed paw reached for us, but Talon was just out of reach. Her clawed forefoot slapped the grizzhorn's arm away, leaving a jagged wound. The grizzhorn pressed the attack, lunging at us again. Talon spun and kicked and caught the grizzhorn in the head. It stood up, roaring. Talon turned again so we were facing it. I fired my rifle, and the rounds struck it in the chest, neck, and head. The headshot put it down. I kept my rifle on it, just in case. The grizzhorn was as big as Talon and weighed more. It was dead, so I stepped down from Talon and checked her for wounds.

Are you hurt?

I don't think so. Are you okay?

Yeah, but I wouldn't be if you had not been so quick. I don't know how I stayed in the saddle.

Talon was not hurt, but there were claw marks on the saddle, a near miss that could have been deadly. I checked the grizzhorn. There were multiple gunshot wounds in it that were not mine. The smell of smoke was stronger here. I mounted, and we followed the smell.

Behind some buildings, we found dead horses and a wagon on its side. I had been concentrating so hard on the grizzhorn that I missed the other mind. It was an unconscious man, probably in or under the wagon.

We circled the wagon. It was obvious the grizzhorn had killed the horses and turned the wagon over. The unconscious man had his legs pinned by the wagon. I dismounted, and Talon pushed the wagon back onto its wheels. I checked the man. He had at least one broken leg and probably some internal injuries. His pupils were the same, so I hoped that meant no concussion. I put him in a deeper sleep and set his leg.

Can you talk to Shep? I didn't want to leave the man to bring Shep and the herd here.

Not like we talk, but I can show visions. I nodded, and unsaddled her.

Go show Shep what happened and have him come here. Talon turned and galloped away, taking my message.

I kept my mind open for anything approaching. All of this blood was going to attract predators. Hopefully, the smell of the grizzhorn would keep most of them away. I started a fire to heat water and cleaned the man's wounds as I waited for it to boil.

It wasn't long before Talon was back. *He comes.*

It took Shep and the herd an hour to arrive. He glanced at the man, and we started setting up camp.

"Grizzhorn, huh?"

I nodded, "Yep."

"Mean things, even at the best of times."

"This was the first one I ever saw up close. The man's bullets wounded it but didn't kill it. I'd hate to meet one in the dark."

"We should skin it and take its head and horns. They say its meat is good too."

"As big as it is, it will take both of us and Talon to do the job."

He thought a moment. "In that case, we'll just take the head and the back strap. The dogs can eat on the carcass for the rest of the time we're here."

It turns out grizzhorn meat is good.

I looked over the man's wagon, checking for damage. For the most part, it was okay. Everything that had been in shelves was now in the floor. All the parts, tools, and equipment were tossed everywhere. From what I could, see he must be a tronics geek of some kind. I picked up the scattered items and put them back in his wagon.

The next morning as breakfast was cooking, I nudged his mind to wake. I poured a cup of coffee and waited.

"Water, please," were his first words. I gave him a cup, and he drank all of it. "Thank you." He looked down at his leg, "How bad is it?"

"Simple fracture, bruises, and some cuts are what I found. How are your ribs?"

"Sore, but not broken." I handed him a cup of coffee. "I take it, since I'm still here, the grizzhorn is dead?"

I nodded, "You put some bullets in him—hurt him pretty bad—but we finished the job."

"I appreciate the help."

I nodded, "What happened?"

He took a swallow of coffee. "I stopped for the day to set up camp, as I wanted to check this place out. I had just unhitched the horses when they must have smelt the grizzhorn and went nuts. Suddenly, it was there and started killing the horses. I got clear of them and got my rifle. I fired a few rounds into him, and he ducked behind the wagon. The next thing I see is the wagon hitting me, and then blackness."

Shep brought us our breakfast of bacon, eggs, and biscuits. "That's the last of the eggs," he said.

The geek took his. "Thanks. They call me Coder."

"I'm Price, and that's Shep." We concentrated on our food for a bit, and I refilled our coffee cups.

"The wagon doesn't look too bad," he said.

"Not too bad, but we'll have to take a closer look," I answered. He was looking us over as he ate, missing little.

"You have quite a herd there."

"We round up mavericks as we travel," I said.

He nodded, "Smart."

I felt no malice from him as we talked, only gratitude. I could tell his pain level was rising. "How's your pain?"

"It's starting to talk to me. I got some pain pills in my wagon, if you'd get them for me."

"It may take some looking, but I'll do it."

He told me what to look for, and I finally found them. He took a pill and went to sleep.

Out of boredom, I put his wagon to rights as well as I could. At least nothing else would get broken in movement. Once I had everything put away, I padded the floor so he would have a comfortable space to travel, as much as possible anyway.

I woke Coder so he could eat lunch. "So, what's the plan?" he asked.

"Well, we're headed for Amarillo. I've got your wagon set up for you to ride in it, and two of our horses can pull it. Once we get there, you can decide what you want to do. Or at any point along the way, if you want to drop off, that's up to you."

"Thank you. I'll buy the horses and chip in on the food as long as my supplies last. Any tronics you have that need fixing, I'll do it for you."

I nodded. "We'll work something out; you just rest. If you don't want to tell me, I'll understand, but what where you looking for here? This place was salvaged years ago."

"Tronics and tronics parts. Very few people mess with them and don't see the value in them," he answered. "Since we're here, if I tell you what I'm looking for, can you look around for me?"

"Sure, I'm always willing to learn how to salvage better."

"Great. First, you'll be looking for a tronics parts store or a tronics repair shop. You know what tronics are, so you'll recognize it when you see it, like the parts you saw in my wagon." I nodded. "I'm not choosy; I'll take any parts you find."

***

I took Talon and rode slowly around town. We did find a tronics repair shop. The roof was still intact, so there may be some good salvage left. Most of the glass front was long gone. I cast my mind around and only felt small animals, mice mostly. I eased my way through the shop, heading toward the back rooms.

In my experience, that was where most shops kept their parts. The shelves in the back were full of items, repaired or waiting to be repaired. They were things no one used anymore because few had electricity.

I looked through the drawers and shelves and found a few things. At the end of the workbench stood a wall cabinet with the doors partially open. Inside were stacks of parts and blank circuit boards. I bagged them and kept looking. There was nothing else worth taking, so I left the shop. I looked around town a little more, but nothing caught my eye until I saw what looked like an old gun sign.

Most of the windows were gone, but a lot of the openings still had bars over them. I cast my mind around, finding only small to medium-sized returns. I stepped through the open door and looked around. The place was trashed. All that was left were empty shelves and broken showcases. The rest of the town was much the same. I went back to the wagons.

"Not much there," I said, handing Coder the bag of parts.

"Thank you," he said, taking the bag. He poured the contents out on his lap. It reminded me of a kid looking through a pile of candy.

"Anything good in there?" I asked.

"Oh yeah, all of this is good. These are common parts in all tronics. I'll put them to good use." I poured two cups of coffee and gave him one. "When you figure on moving on?" he asked.

"I thought we'd give you a day or two more for that leg to set in place, and then move on."

"I appreciate that, but when you're ready, I am. I got my pain pills, so I'll be alright."

"No rush. We'll let the cattle rest here and fatten up a bit. No harm done."

Over a supper of biscuits, beans, and grizzhorn, we talked of the places and things we had seen.

"I see where Shepard got his handle. That one is kind of obvious. How'd you come by, Price?"

I smiled. "The old man at our town's trading post, Junker, gave it to me. He said all I ever did when I went in there was ask the price of everything in the store, so he started calling me Price. The joke was on him, though, because I memorized the price of everything he ever sold. After that, he never got the better of me on a deal. How about you? All I ever heard a tronics geek called was geek-something."

He nodded. "I am not only a geek; I'm a coder. I write tronics language, the language that makes tronics do things. I just don't get to use it much. Most everything I find just needs a part replaced to fix it. I got bored moving from town to town fixing stereos, so I came out on the frontier for some excitement. I think this was a case of, 'Be careful what you ask for because you may get it.' I don't think I'll ever complain about being bored again, out loud anyway."

For the next few days, I rode the area picking up mavericks to add to our herd. Shep brought up a cow that had a calf so Coder could have milk to help his broken leg heal.

CHAPTER 5

Talon and I rode out a few miles and scouted the area. I scanned the region with my eyes and mind. All we found were the normal animals for there. Shep had set up under some trees to keep the camp cool in the hot weather. When we rode up, Coder was working on the refrigerators. I unsaddled Talon and let her loose.

"The leg feeling better?" I asked, as I leaned in to see what he was fixing.

"Yeah, but I'm still taking it easy," he said, looking at his test meter.

"Something wrong with the frig?" I asked, watching as the test meter numbers changed.

"No, I was looking at the circuit they used building this. I think I can improve on the design and make the frig more efficient," he said, putting his meter down.

"That would be great. What do you need to do it?"

"I have everything I need. Those new boards you found will be the base for the design change. Whoever built this didn't have the right size boards, so he used three rather than one. I can do more with the one I have."

"We'll be building more wagons like this one to sell, so keep some boards to use on the next one. I'll pay you for your work."

"Brother, I'll be repaying you for a while," he said.

"How long before you can make the improvement?"

"Already done. The solar panel will give a better charge using less sunlight, and the batteries will be more efferent."

"Wow, you work fast."

"I didn't want my work to hold up your move."

"You think your leg can stand moving tomorrow?"

"I think so. I'm ready to try."

"Alright, we'll plan to move in the morning."

We packed his wagon up that night so he would be ready. That way Shep could concentrate on our wagon and breakfast.

After supper, we sat around the fire and listened to Shep play and sing to our cattle.

"That is the most amazing thing I have ever seen," Coder said.

"Yeah, he's good. I've never seen anything like it either. Sure saves a lot of work," I said, smiling.

"Do you think you could look at my PK data-pad? The screen's been blinking while I'm typing."

"Sure, I enjoy checking code more than soldering parts." I pulled the data-pad out of my bag, unlocked it with my finger print, and handed it to him. "Oh, yeah. Come to papa," he said. I chuckled.

I poured myself another cup of coffee while Coder focused in. I thought he was talking in code.

"Uh-huh, yep that's right. No, let's change that." He stopped and looked up at me. "What rank did you say you were? Sargent?"

"Yeah, why?"

"I think this is an officer's data-pad. It has a lot of capabilities but very few are turned on. And did you know they can track you?"

"What do you mean, track me?"

"This data-pad is turned on to send location updates to wherever headquarters is."

"Can you tell where headquarters is?"

"No, it just sends out a signal. When the signal is picked up, it forwards it somewhere. I'd have to be at one of those receiving stations."

"Can you see who else is being tracked?"

"Let me see what I can do." He put his head down over the screen and went to typing.

I drank another cup of coffee while he worked. There was no talking this time.

"I need to go to my wagon and get some more equipment."

I helped him to his wagon, and he turned his equipment on. He had a battery system running his equipment. No wonder he knew what to do on the frig systems. Once everything was powered up, he plugged my data-pad into it and went back to work. After a while, I got tired of watching, went back to the fire, and then to my blankets.

We were up at sunrise. Well, Shep and I were. Coder was still up working.

"We moving?" Shep asked.

"Let's wait and see what Coder has found, then decide." He nodded and started breakfast.

When coffee was ready, I poured two cups and walked over to Coder's wagon. I looked in the back, and he had my data-pad taken apart and all kinds of wires plugged into it.

"If you break, it you buy it," I said.

"Uh-huh," was all he said. He did take the cup of coffee though.

Just before lunch, he called out, "Price."

I went over to see what he had. "You find something?"

"Yes. As far as I can tell, they keep track of everyone. The information is sent back east. That's the best I can tell using what I have here. Some of the data-pads, like yours, are capable of sending messages and what are called emails."

"What's email?"

"It's like a letter sent over the data-pad to other data-pads."

"Can you tell who the data-pads are assigned to? "

"Sure, or what name they are using."

"Can you tell where a Captain Vance is?"

He typed a little. "Yep," and he turned the screen to show me. The screen was a U. S. map. We enlarged it to get a better idea of exactly where he was.

"East Texas," I said. "I wonder if he knows he's being tracked. I doubt he does, or I think he would have mentioned it. I can understand headquarters wanting to keep track of their people, but why hide it?"

"Do you want to ask him?"

"Yeah, when I see him, we'll have a long talk."

Coder chuckled. "No, do you want to ask him now?"

"We can do that?"

"We can now; I hacked their system. You can message anyone who has the same system as yours and send emails to anyone. They just won't get the email until they log in and update."

"If we do, will anyone but us see the message?"

"Possible, but not likely. It's code blocked."

"Okay, message him, but let's be careful. If this is nothing, I don't want anyone getting into trouble. If it's something, I don't want them knowing we know."

He nodded. "Okay, what do you want to say?"

I thought a moment. "Twisted Knee, this is the drifter. Did you know we are being tracked using our data-pads?"

He sent the message. "It may be a while before he replies."

"Okay, let's eat lunch." We didn't get a reply until that evening.

"Drifter, I did not. Is this a closed loop?"

"Yes, so my new friend tells me. He's a geek, saw we were being tracked."

"Can he turn off the tracking?"

Coder nodded. "He says he can."

"Can he turn off all, some, or just one?"

"All, any, or one," Coder said as I typed.

"If you shut me down, can I still get messages?"

Coder nodded. "He says, yes."

"Turn my locator off and leave everyone else's on, just in case someone gets suspicious."

I handed Coder my data-pad. He typed, and handed it back to me. "Off," he said.

"He says you are now off."

"Good, I'm going to investigate, quietly. I'll try to find out what's going on. Hopefully nothing."

"Just remember what our friend said about him following you. He might have lied about his info," I wrote.

"I was wondering the same thing."

"Watch your back."

"U2."

Coder took the data-pad. "I've added code blockers to your pad. No one will be able to tell your settings have changed, or that you sent a message. When you update, it will all look the same as before. If a program tries to change it, it will seem to them that it changed, but your pad is locked and will not change."

I nodded, "Good, let's hope this is all just old news that no one uses anymore." I don't think either of us believed that.

"Coder, would you keep watch on the pad for any activity that may show up, and if any other pads get close to us?"

"Sure, no problem."

"We pull out tomorrow morning. You'd better get some sleep," I said.

"That sounds like good advice; I think I'll follow it." And with that, he went to his wagon and turned in.

***

We pulled out the next morning but travelled slowly to see how Coder was going to handle the first day. He did okay but took pain pills at noon. He moved a little slower around camp that night and went to his wagon early.

We travelled easy over the next week. Eventually, Coder no longer needed to take pain pills to make it through the day. He moved around better but still went to his wagon early in the evenings. Shep was making sure he got plenty of milk, too, and always kept some in the frig. The frig was working much better with Coder's improvements. Things stayed colder and froze better, and the batteries now stayed fully charged.

Coder was not a burden around camp. Anything he could do to help he did. In the evenings, he taught me about my data-pad and all that it could do. He taught Shep and I how to use a test meter and what to look for when troubleshooting tronics. We were far from experts, but we could do basic checks.

We kept picking up mavericks as we moved. We also did

some business, trading with the farms and ranches we passed. When folks found out we had a geek with us, Coder picked up some work.

We stayed at the Redmond's pig farm a few days, killing and packing pork. He traded us his pork to resupply his farm. He also got some beef, and we helped him butcher them. Coder hung right in there with us, doing what he could, and never complained.

Talon even got in on the action. The farmer needed his cold root cellar expanded, so Talon put those big claws to work. What would have taken us a day or two, she had done in only a few hours. She did the rough heavy work; we did the fine finish work. For her efforts, I gave her a bath and washed her down good. She loved the attention.

The night before we left, Shep and the farmer's wife cooked up a feast. We all ate like it was the Fourth of July. We talked as we ate.

"Now this is how it's supposed to be, folks helping folks," the farmer said.

I nodded. "Yes sir, if we could get back to that belief, we'd all be doing better. My grandpa told me that was the way it was in what he called 'back in the day'. Said neighbors help neighbors. It made everyone's life easier."

"Well, anytime you fellers are by this way, you stop in. You're always welcome. If you make this part of a supply route, count us in as customers."

"We'll do that. I think we'll both make money off this trade. I'd like to buy a few hogs to see how they move along with our herd."

"They should do all right; hogs can cover a lot of territory when they want to."

Shep had already told me they'd be no problem. He had moved hogs before. When we pulled out the next morning, we had four hogs as part of our herd, which gave me the idea of calling up wild hogs. But that might be asking for trouble.

***

We kept a good pace, heading toward Amarillo. We did some small business on a few farmsteads and ranches, but nothing major. I kept our larders full, using fresh game as we moved.

The night before we arrived in Amarillo, we discussed our plans.

"Once we get into Amarillo, we'll sell all our livestock and resupply the wagon. I'm thinking of crossing back over into Oklahoma and working back down the Red to bring in mavericks on the way to OKCF. Coder, you're welcome to ride along if you're a mind to. Unless you want to go your own way or stay in Amarillo."

"If you don't mind a banged-up geek tagging along, I wouldn't mind. I'm not interested in staying in Amarillo."

I nodded, "Shep, what are your thoughts?"

"That sounds fine to me."

"When we get there, I'm going to go check in at the PK office. Coder, why don't you come with me and look at their equipment."

"I'd love to. That will tell me what I'm up against."

We relaxed the rest of the evening, listening to Shep play his guitar and sing. Shep had made bear-sign and coffee. If I'm not careful, I'm going to get fat following Shep around, but they sure were good.

We were up with the dawn. Breakfast was coffee and the rest of the bear-sign. We were on the move an hour later. The road was clear and smooth, so we made good time.

Our first stop was the stockyards. We sold all of our stock there, including the hogs, which had had no problem travelling right along with us.

We rented a yard inside the wall for our wagons and stock, unhitched everything, and cared for our animals. Shep and the dogs took first watch on the wagon, while Coder and I went to the PK office.

This office, which was close to the gate, didn't have a full time PK on duty. There was a palm pad on the door. I set my hand to it, and after a few moments, it beeped, turned green, and the door opened. We went inside and shut the door behind us. I didn't want any interruptions.

It was a standard, barebones office with a one-way window looking out. We could see out, but no one could see in. I docked my data-pad, and we watched the screen as it updated the information.

Coder followed the cables around, and I heard him say, "The server must be in here."

The door was locked. Coder took a keypad out of his bag and plugged into the door's palm pad. I watched him work. In less than a minute, he had the door open. We stepped inside and closed the door. Coder walked around, looking at everything.

"The server is a standard server, but the encoding equipment is not. This must be special for a PK."

We walked to the rear of the room where the repair station was. "Whoa, now that's a repair station. They have everything they need to completely rebuild pads, PCs, servers, any piece of equipment they have." Coder was like a kid in a candy store. "Judging by the stacks of unrepaired gear, I'd say they don't have anyone who knows how to do the work."

He looked through the equipment that was awaiting repair. Most of it was data-pads. "According to the dates on the repair requests, it's been years since anyone has worked on any of these."

He went to the server station, sat down, and began typing. I had an idea but needed to make sure I could do what I wanted to do. I opened my data-pad and looked under the heading: "Additional Duties and Responsibilities of a PK". Then I looked under "Authorities of a PK". I finally found what I was looking for.

I, as a PK Sargent, could hire either full-time or temporary workers in the pursuit of my duties. I could also "swear in" a new member to the PK. I had to ensure they completed the PK training. A PK geek, or what they called an "I. T. Tech," did not usually work out on the range. He usually worked at stations and offices. Their pay scale was the same as a Scout's. I nodded, thinking.

"Washington D. C.," Coder said, looking at the screen and

typing.

"What about it?" I asked, walking over to see what he was talking about.

"That's where the tracking information is going. So far, I can't tell you any closer than Washington D. C." He kept typing.

"I'm guessing PK Headquarters, Washington D. C."

"Hold on. Washington is sending a feed to New York and Dallas. Maybe they are regional headquarters?" he asked.

"Maybe. I'm still going to act as if we are in enemy territory."

"I agree. When in doubt, err on the side of safety. You live longer that way."

"How would you like access to this workshop, and others like it, and make money to boot?"

He turned to look at me. "Will it get me hung?"

"I don't think so. If you do, I'll make sure they use a new rope," I said, smiling. "According to the PK Laws and Rule Book, I am authorized to hire you, or swear you in as a PK Geek. It pays the same as a PK Scout."

He thought a moment. "What would I have to do?"

"Well, to start with, PK Geeks don't normally work out in the field. They work at a station or office. They aren't usually needed all the time, so you work like a Scout. That would give you a paycheck during hard times and room and board while active. I could do your basic training to activate you. That would allow you to use and relocate any of this equipment you need to do your job."

His eyes ran over all the tronics gear and parts in the room.

"Any equipment?"

"Whatever you need to do your job. And your first task would be to fix a data-pad for yourself."

"And a laptop. I would need a PC and some other equipment."

I smiled. "And a laptop, PC, and anything else you need to do your job. And take enough parts with us to completely rebuild and update, or upgrade, Captain Vance's data-pad. Ours, too, for that matter."

"What rank would I be?"

"Well, I can only make you a Corporal. However, when we meet Captain Parker, we'll have him make you a Sargent. I'm sure once he sees what you can do, he'll promote you."

"It's tempting; let me think about it."

"We'll stay here a few days. If you decide to join, we may stay a few days longer so you can work here and fix some of this stuff to prove your worth, in case someone take an interest."

"Okay, I'll let you know for sure tomorrow."

I nodded, "Let's go relieve Shep."

CHAPTER 6

I stayed with the wagon and ate, while Shep and Coder went looking around. The dogs stayed with me, or rather the wagon. They were both back early, so I went to get a haircut, bath, and dinner. After the haircut and bath, I felt much better. I found a steakhouse and ate there. It wasn't bad, but it didn't hold a candle to Miss Ruth's.

I started to feel strained, or antagonistic, feelings close by. There were three cowboys at a table in the corner. They seemed to be the source. I shifted my feet to a better position, just in case I had to move quickly.

One of them stood up unsteadily and staggered toward me. He put his hand on my table to balance himself. He was dressed like he had just come in off the range.

"I hate Peacekeepers," he said. His two friends snickered, and he looked around at them, smiling.

"I know what you mean. There are some I don't like myself." He stared at me, blinking. He hadn't expected that. I didn't give him time to think, not that he was thinking too clearly anyway. "How's the roundup going?" I asked, as I cut another bite off my steak.

"Not bad, they ain't too bad scattered." He pulled out a chair and sat down.

"Yeah, I just brought a herd in; they stayed close." Of course, I had Shep to keep them that way.

"I thought you was a PK?" He looked at me through bleary eyes.

"Part time, I'm a Scout. They call me when they need me. Some of them boys couldn't find their butt with both hands in their back pockets. When I'm not scouting, I do some trading and cattle wrangling to make do."

"Yeah, sometimes it's hand-to-mouth."

"It is for a fact."

I kept sending him calming thoughts and telling him to go to sleep. I watched his so-called friends out of the corner of my eye and kept eating. He lay his head down on the table and went to sleep. I finished and paid my tab. I wasn't on active duty, so this time dinner was on me.

I walked by the table where the two "friends" sat. "Next time you tough men want to have some fun, why don't you go find a little girl's hair to pull. That seems more your speed."

The big one jumped up, and I caught him with a short jab to his temple. He dropped like a bag of rocks. His friend was coming up with his hand on his knife.

"If you pull it, I'll kill ya." My hand was down by my pistol. He let go of his knife like a hot coffee pot handle. "Wake your other friend up, and y'all get this idiot home to sleep it off. This is the end. If you come looking for more, it won't end with one punch."

He nodded, and I watched him roust the other. Satisfied that it was over for now, I left.

I strolled back to the wagon and got my bedroll out where I could get to it when I was ready. Shep had a pot of coffee on and was strumming his guitar. I poured me a cup and sat down. No one spoke. We just enjoyed a quiet evening.

***

"When can I start?" Coder said over his breakfast cup of coffee and plates of eggs.

"Today if you want." I took another swallow of coffee. "The geek stuff you know. You just have to read their PK rules on the subject. Now that I think about it, you should read these first. I don't really know that much about it, and you don't want to find out about bad stuff after I swear you in. We'll be doing enough bad stuff anyway," I said, smiling.

"You are so funny. Besides, I already read the PK rules and regulations covering I. T. Tech duties and responsibilities."

"Okay, after we finish eating, we can go to the office and do the paperwork."

He nodded, "Sounds good. Then I can check out my new toys." I nodded, chuckling.

Shep started doing maintenance of the wagon, while we went to the PK Office. We went inside, Coder filled out the paperwork, and I gave him his Oath of Enlistment into the Peacekeepers.

He wasted no time and went straight to work on the broken, or "non-operational," equipment, as he called it. The first thing he did was find himself the best data-pad that was there and upgraded it. Then, he upgraded mine as well.

After looking through every storage cabinet in the shop, he found a test laptop. "This will do for a start. I'll trade up as we check the other PK sites."

We stayed in Amarillo for a week while Coder finished repairing all of the broken equipment. When he was done, he made a spare parts kit for his wagon. I don't know what all he took, but it's not my job. He's the PK Geek.

Shep resupplied our wagon, and we were once again on the trail. We crossed the Red River heading back into Oklahoma, then turned southeast. We didn't start gathering mavericks until we were a few days out from Amarillo. We stayed close to the Red, as the cattle were going to need the water.

There seemed to be more cattle on the Oklahoma side of the Red than the Texas side. Shep and his dogs were doing a good business, and our herd grew daily.

Talon and I roved out and around, scouting as we moved. I was able to take a deer, or a hog every couple of days, which stretched our supplies. Coder helped around the camp anyway he could and worked on his tronics in the evening. We didn't rush any morning, as we wanted fat cattle. We ate breakfast, packed up, and moved on. Shep had made sandwiches for lunch, so our stop would be brief.

I smell smoke Talon sent.

Close or far?

Not too far. On the wind from across the river.

"I smell smoke. Ain't the Redmond's place about here across the river?" I asked.

Shep nodded, looking south. "About there, yeah." Coder was looking south too.

"I'm going to ride that way to see if I see anything. Y'all keep moving, and I'll catch up."

On impulse, I pulled my AR-10 case out of the wagon and slipped it into my saddle straps. The case was waterproof, so it was safe if we had to cross the river. We took off, following the smell of smoke.

We rode along the river for a bit, and then saw smoke rising. From the amount of smoke, it was probably a building of some kind—a house or barn.

We crossing?

Yes, it might be the Redmond's place.

Talon swam better than a normal horse. She used her forefeet to pull us along, and we had no trouble crossing. As we approached, I felt several minds, men and horses. It was the Redmond's place all right, and it was their barn burning. We circled around, staying downwind because of scent and sound. This way I could hear them better.

Three of the men were on their horses out front. I was to their side.

"You can come out and give us what we want or stay in there and burn."

That was all I needed to hear. I dismounted and got the AR-10 out and screwed on its suppressor. The suppressor would cut down my range, but at two hundred yards it wouldn't matter. I threw my scout cape on and got ready.

There had been no reply from the house. I sighted in on the riders. The wind was still, but heat was rising from the ground. I sent to their horses not to move; they were safe. I fired two rounds back-to-back. The first round went through the first rider and into the second, killing both. The second round killed the third rider. The three fell from their horses, and the horses didn't move.

There were six more men posted surrounding the house. All their horses were in one place away from the house and burning barn.

Go get those horses. I sent Talon an image of the ones I wanted. *Bring them back over here.* She turned and moved off, heading around toward them.

One of the men was moving back toward me, trying to see what had happened. As soon as I had a clear shot, I put him down. I waited a moment, and no one else moved. I started circling to get into a new shooting position. I had fired three rounds from here. It was time to move.

Talon was heading back with the rest of the horses.

Keep them back over there, I'll be back. I got a mental nod from her.

I silently eased up on the next man, and when I was close enough, I crushed his brain stem. He never even made a sound. I continued around the circle. I wondered if there was a way I could put someone out without killing him. I thought about the guy I had punched in the temple the other night.

I was close to the next man, so I concentrated on his temple. I formed a thought in my mind of a punch and to "punch" him in the temple. Nothing happened. Well, he did shake his head. I tried it again, putting more effort into the "punch." He dropped where he was.

I waited. He was out cold. I moved toward him, focused, and put him into a deep sleep. I moved on around the circle and "punched" the last three in their temples, knocking them out and putting them to sleep.

I went toward the off side of the house. "Mr. Redmond, this is PK Scout Sargent Price. Can you hear me?"

"I hear you," came a response.

"I've taken care of the marauders. I'm stepping out, and I'd appreciate it if you don't shoot me. Also, if your wife has any of that apple pie left, I'll take a slice."

"You must be crazy. That pie didn't make it to sundown," I heard him laugh.

I took my cape off, lay the AR down, and stepped out with both hands out to my sides.

He recognized me and opened the front door. "Scout, you are a sight for sore eyes. I don't know what brought you back, but we sure appreciate you."

"We're were moving down the other side of the river and saw the smoke. Thought I'd come see if you needed a hand. Everyone all right?"

"Yeah, we got inside before they could do more than fire the barn."

"Good, barns can be replaced, but people can't."

"Amen to that."

"I'm going back out to collect my trash. I'll be back after a while."

"Need any help?"

"No, you stay with your family. I'll take care of this PK business."

He nodded and went back inside.

I had Talon bring the horses in. I tied the bodies and the" sleepers" over their saddles. Then, we went back out in front to where the three leaders were. Now that I was close, I recognized them. They were the three cowboys from the restaurant in Amarillo. I just shook my head, tied them over their saddles, and moved them well away from the house.

I took all their prints and pictures. Four of them had a hundred-dollar price on their heads. I made two hundred dollars this afternoon. I searched all the men and put everything of value in a pile. Next, I looked through their saddlebags. There was one hundred twenty-seven dollars between them. They all had decent guns, rifles, and saddles. The horses were good stock as well. In one of the saddlebags, I found a PK data-pad. I set it to the side and packed everything back into the saddlebags.

After laying out the four sleepers, I made sure they were tied securely. Then I reached into their minds and woke them up. It took them a few minutes to become coherent, but as soon as they were, they started fighting their ropes. They kicked, spit, cussed, and screamed; I let them fight until they gave out.

One started crying. He would be the weakest link, so I'd save him for last. I held the data-pad I had found in the saddlebag in my hand and walked down the line showing them the pad.

"The first one to tell me all about this PK data-pad won't hang."

"We ain't telling you nothing."

I drew my right-hand pistol and shot him in the leg. He screamed and started cussing me.

"You didn't let me finish. As I was saying, the first one to tell me all about this PK data-pad won't hang. The rest of you will die painfully."

"We ain't telling you squat," Wounded Leg said.

He was a tough old bird; I'll give him that. I drew my left-hand pistol and shot him through the ankle. He screamed and passed out.

I held the pad in front of the next man, but he said nothing. I shot him in the knee. He screamed.

"Wait," the third man said, "you didn't even ask anything."

"I'm sorry; this is like a wedding. Speak now or forever hold your peace, or at least until you get tired of the pain."

"It was Caster that killed him," Crying Man said.

"Go on."

"About a year ago we were raiding a herd. The PK caught up with us a few days later. We got the drop on him. Castor said we needed to make an example out of him. He cut him up bad, just to hear him scream, then hung him slow to watch him kick."

My anger went dark. "Which one is Castor?"

"The first one you shot." I nodded, drew, and shot crying man in the head, killing him instantly.

I waited for Castor to wake up. He spit blood where he had chewed his tongue. "You'd better kill me PK 'cause, if I get loose, I'm gonna take a week to kill you."

"We'll get to that in a minute. They tell me you're a real bad man. You like to torture and make examples of your enemies."

He laughed, "That's right. What you gonna do? Hang me?" he snorted.

I laughed with him; he stopped. "Oh, I'm going to hang you...eventually," I laughed, leaving that unknown hanging there in the air.

I went back to the Redmond place. The barn fire was mostly out by the time I got back. They were outside watching to make sure nothing else caught on fire.

"Mr. Redmond, if you will bury these, you can have their horses, guns, and saddles. You can also have all the rest of the guns. These boys won't be needing them. Sell what you don't want for yourselves to pay to replace your barn." I handed him the one hundred twenty-seven dollars. "This was all the cash they had on them. It should help too."

He took it and looked at the horses. "Thank you, Scout. This should pay for a new barn and then some."

"Will you stay for supper, Sargent Price? I've made another apple pie," Mrs. Redmond said.

"No, ma'am, we have an appointment in Amarillo we need to get to. I appreciate the invite though. Next time for sure."

***

We rode straight through to Amarillo, their hands tied behind their backs and to the saddle. When we arrived, I took them to the newspaper office. The newsman came outside.

"I'm about to hang what's left of a marauders gang. If you want to get your camera, I'll give you a story to print to go with the pictures." He ran back inside and got his camera.

"We don't get a last meal?" one of the marauders asked.

"Do I look that generous to you?"

I took them to the closest tree and threw ropes over the limbs.

"Any last words?" I mocked.

Castor spit at me. I led his horse slowly out from under him, but his neck didn't break. It took him a while to choke to death.

I looked at the other two. "Any last words?"

"Just make it clean," one said, and the other nodded. Their horses lunged from under them and, at the same time, I crushed their brain stem. They were dead before the ropes tightened.

The newsman got his pictures and the story.

"What are you, the Grim Reaper?" he asked.

"Nope, just a reaper. If you kill a Peacekeeper, that is an automatic death sentence. It took us a year to find them, but we finally did. There they hang."

The pictures and the article went everywhere. However, my picture was not included.

***

I sold the horses and tack to the stables; I didn't need them. I paid the undertaker to cut them down after dark and bury them. The public hanging had served its purpose. Hanging them where no one saw was not a warning to anyone.

When I caught up with Shep and Coder, we stopped for the day. They had been moving slowly, increasing our herd. I brushed Talon down and let her rest. We had been on the move for almost five days, and we both needed a break.

We all rested, and I filled them in on all that had happened. I gave Coder the PK data-pad I took from Castor. "If you would, check this out and tell me everything you can about it, especially if you can track its movements."

"Okay, it will take me a day or so."

I nodded, "No problem."

"You would think, after all this time, people would learn. Marauders don't live long, and there are plenty of ways to make a living," Coder said.

"There has always been lazy, trashy people who would rather steal what you have than work. They don't think far enough ahead to see the final cost of the seeds they sow," Shep said.

I nodded, "And mercy is hard to come by these days. When

the account comes due, it can come hard."

With that, I found my blankets and turned in early for the night. Reaping is hard work, but someone has to do it.

***

"Grandpa, what did the preacher mean when he said we live in a cast-down world?"

"Well, part of that comes from the Bible. The Bible says this is a fallen world. In another place, it speaks of angels being cast down to earth, or cast out of Heaven. I think he just put those things together."

"I don't understand. Why would he think the world was cast down? Cast down from where?"

The old man chuckled. "Well, that goes back, according to the Bible, to before Adam and Eve. God made the world perfect, but because of disobedience the world fell and became imperfect. That's what the preacher mean by this being a fallen world."

"Okay, but why a cast-down world?"

"That's because of the comet, or the asteroid, Wormwood. Wormwood is also mentioned in the Bible. When Wormwood made its close pass to earth, it changed the world overnight—earthquakes, tidal waves, power grid failures, epidemics, mutations, the list goes on. We literally went from a relatively peaceful, prosperous world to a world at war with itself overnight. Human nature being what it is, the strong started preying on the weak, and only the strong survived."

"Society is just now starting to turn back to the rule of law. We're not there yet, as it's still up to the individual to enforce the law. If you are wronged, it's up to you to make it right. As a personal choice, I consider it an obligation to help protect the weaker in our society, especially women and children."

"We, here at least, have reverted to what they called the 'law of the west', or Western Justice. There was an old saying, 'We stomp our own snakes,' meaning we took care of our own problems. If you wrong us, we'll make it right, even if blood is shed. We don't back down. That is another reason we train so hard."

"Preacher said God has turned His back on us."

"Now, me and the preacher differ on that. If God had turned His back on us, we would all be dead. It is only by the grace of God that any of us are alive. It's good we have a preacher, but preachers are human, and humans make mistakes. That is why it's important to read the Bible for yourself. Don't blindly follow anyone. Judge for yourself, based on God's word."

CHAPTER 7

When I woke, the memory of my grandfather made me smile. I could almost hear him, *"Get moving boy; we're burning day-light."*

Our days got back to normal for trail days. We eased along the old Forty-Four Trail through Lawton and Chickasha, continued gathering and fattening cattle, and traded when we got the opportunity. The weather had taken it easy on us, nothing extreme. We did get rain, but it was slow, easy, and didn't last long. That helped the grass grow, which also helped our cattle.

We had finished dinner, Shep was singing the cattle down, and we were enjoying coffee.

"I finally got into the data-pad from the dead PK. I found some odd things," Coder piped up.

"What kind of odd things?"

"I was able to track its movement, but I don't know who had it during the middle part of the movement."

"Okay, what's odd about that?"

"Someone went to City-Fort Orleans, but I can't tell who. If it was the PK, he didn't check in. If it was, what was his name, Castor? That's kind of odd for a cowboy marauder."

I nodded, thinking. "What was the PK's name?"

"PK Jim Rojas."

"Anything about him?"

"Not really. This was his first trip out alone with no partner."

"How long did he stay in Orleans?"

"Six days, but he stayed within a half day's ride of it for another three days before heading back west."

"Sounds like he was meeting someone. Was it a PK just going to Orleans because he wanted to? Why wait three days outside the city? If it was Castor, was the marauder spending his spoils? That doesn't sound right. They usually spend their money at the first gaming house they come to."

"Orleans has plenty of those, so I hear," he said, smiling. Shep chuckled.

"Does that show an exact location?" Shep asked.

"Pretty close, fifty-meter grid," Coder answered.

"Can you show me?" Shep asked.

"Sure." Coder pulled up the map and handed the pad to Shep.

He looked, expanding it and zooming in. "That area is not where you would normally find someone like a marauder. That's where people with money go to play. Too rich for me."

"So, if they weren't playing, they were there meeting someone, someone with money," I said.

"Or power and influence," Shep added.

"Which makes this even more of a mystery."

"I wonder if Captain Vance knew Rojas. Send him an email with all the information we have about this. Perhaps he has some insights."

Coder put an email together and sent it. I retired to bed early.

***

I had kept Mandy's signing book for a week. I didn't really need it, as I had it memorized the first day. I didn't want them to know how fast I could learn things, so I kept it longer. Mandy was waiting on their porch as I walked up. I set the book down and signed.

°Not a lot of words in the book, is there another one?°

Mandy's face split into a smile. °Yes, there are other books. That was just the first one. Are you ready for the second?°

°Yes, I need more words, so I can understand and talk with you better.°

I handed her the book, and she took it inside. She returned with the second one and handed it to me.

°Would you like to practice signing for a little while?° she signed.

°Sure, I don't have to go right back home.°

We sat on the porch and practiced. I was slow to start but was improving. I could tell Mandy was enjoying signing with someone other than her mother.

Before I was finished, I had memorized eight books, keeping each one a week. I was still slow and sometimes used the wrong word, but I was getting better.

Mandy and I spent more and more time together, signing. She didn't have many friends, well, any would be closer to the truth. Everyone thought less of her because she couldn't talk. Signing with her confirmed what I suspected. She was smart and had a thirst to learn.

Sitting on her porch in the shade, she had a far off look in her eye. °I want to learn to fight. Can you teach me?°

I stared at her a moment. °You don't want one of the instructors to teach you?°

°No, you are a good fighter, and you understand me.° She hesitated, °I trust you.°

°Why now, other than we can sign?°

She looked away, thinking. Making up her mind, she signed, °Mother says I must learn everything I can to overcome my lack of voice. If I want to attract a husband, I must offer him more than just keeping a home—more than cooking, cleaning, washing, and having children. I must make them look past that I am mute.° She watched my reaction.

I nodded, °I'll teach you all I know about fighting, but if they can't see that your lack of voice is only a small part of you, they don't deserve you.°

She smiled and kissed me on the cheek.

I started spending an hour after school, teaching her "our dance." She was graceful, fluid, and quick. She wasn't quite as quick as I was, but quicker than anyone else I had sparred with.

One day, she was looking at the bone scales on my hand. "Comes in handy," I said. She nodded.

°Anywhere else?° she signed.

°Yeah, forearms, shins, knees, neck, spine, ankles, and feet. They protect striking points and bones close to the surface of the skin.°

°Keep a secret?° she signed. I nodded.

She showed me the tip of her finger. As I watched, a cat-like claw extended from under her fingernail. She watched again to see my reaction.

I smiled, "Awesome, do all of your fingers have them?" She smiled, nodding and extending all ten claws. "Feet too?" She nodded. "That is so cool. How strong are they? Can you use them to climb?"

She shrugged. "You haven't tried?" She shook her head. "Oh, I see, you're keeping them secret." She nodded. "I get it. I'll keep your secret, but you need to try them. You need to know what you are capable of in case you need to use them in an emergency." She nodded again.

I looked closer at her claws. "You could do serious damage to someone with these. That's good."

I started teaching her to move in the woods and hunt. She was a fast learner, and it was easier because we enjoyed each other's company.

When I hunted, I always brought extra game home for Mandy and her mother. I made sure they always had fresh meat. I wasn't the best hunter in our clan, but our two families never went hunger because I missed an opportunity.

***

I had killed a hog and was dressing it out to get it ready for the smokehouse.

"Good looking hog," the old man said, walking over.

"Yeah, got him down by the river. Dressed out at over a hundred pounds, I bet."

"Looks like." He helped me with the cleaning and butchering. "You still working with Mandy, teaching her?"

"Yes, sir, the funny thing is I've gotten better by teaching her."

"Yep, that's how it works. You improve by teaching others. She seems a fine young lady."

"She is, and smart as a whip too." The old man nodded. "The clan still does arranged marriages, doesn't it?"

"Sometimes, not as much as they use to," he answered.

I nodded. "How does it work?" We flipped the hog over and continued to work.

"Usually, the two fathers meet informally to see if there is an interest. If there is, they set up another meeting to discuss dowry, when, where, those kinds of things."

"How old do they have to be?"

"No set rule. Some families have made arrangements when they were children."

"So, I'm of age?"

"Yep, you're near fifteen. You got anyone in mind?" he asked, smiling.

I shook my head. "Nope, just wondering?" I said, smiling.

"Well, if you think of someone, you let me know. I'll speak to her father," he said, chuckling.

I stopped. "What if her father is...?"

He nodded. "Then I'll speak to her mother. Don't worry; we'll take care of it." I nodded.

We carried the meat to the smokehouse and hung it. Then we started a low fire outside in the fireplace. Smoke and heat went in through vents in the back of it. We'd have to keep the low fire going for a few days, and then put the meat in the salt chests.

"What about her mother? She doesn't have anyone but Mandy," I said.

He thought a moment. "You could take her in as part of your family, or someone will take her as wife. She's still young yet. We'll figure something out."

I nodded.

"Have you and Mandy talked about this?"

"No, sir, not yet."

"That's your first step. Make sure she's agreeable. She might have her eye on some other feller"

I smiled. "Might."

***

We were on the move again shortly after breakfast. The countryside was a deep green from the rain we had gotten. It was good for the cattle, but the thick undergrowth could also hide more dangers. I was fortunate being able to feel the minds of animals that might be lying in wait. Riding Talon helped too. Few things passed her notice.

My mind drifted, thinking of the dreams I'd been having. I always thought of Mandy, but never this vividly. I stopped on a rise and looked back over our herd. I had done well in the past few months. I had a herd of cattle, working trade wagon, working wagon station, and a sizable bank account. By anyone's standards, I was well off.

I looked off to the east as if I could see home. I sat there for a time and thought. When the herd got closer, I got back to work scouting. It doesn't pay to spend too much time daydreaming on the frontier.

We moved on for the rest of the day and camped at a small copse of trees for the night. Shep made a thick meat stew and some fresh bread. As usual, it was delicious.

I was still thinking of home, listening to Shep sing the cows down. The sight of that still made me smile. I had changed a lot in the past few months. I had never been much for hanging around people, but Shep and Coder were different. They weren't just people; they were friends, companions.

"I've been thinking," I said.

"Is that a new sensation for you?" Coder asked. Shep chuckled.

I smiled. "Not the thinking part, but speaking them aloud is kinda new. I've been thinking it's time for me to make a trip home. I haven't been back in a good while. I've done well for myself, and I'd like to take a herd home, maybe set up a home ranch. And I'd like you both to consider coming with me. I'll need you if I move a herd of any size."

"Where's home?" Coder asked.

"Fort Smith way, a bit east actually. Good valley land there. Cattle do well. When I left, there were no ranches of any size."

"I'm in," Shep said. "Makes no difference to me which way we travel. I just like travelling."

Coder shrugged. "Sure, why not? Never been there before."

"Good, we'll stop in OKC, sell the older stock, and resupply the wagon for the trip into Tulsa. Maybe by the time we get to City-Fort Tulsa, Ben will have another wagon and team ready to sell. We may take two wagons on this trip."

"Not a bad thought," Shep said. "This may start you a wagon supply route that we could keep going."

I nodded in agreement. A dedicated wagon supply route servicing the town, farms, and ranches between forts was a great idea.

"Shep, I'd like you to put some thought into what we might take in the second wagon if we take one. I don't think just taking twice as much would be the best use of the extra cargo."

He nodded. "I'll think on her."

The conversation died there, and I watched the stars cross the sky for a while, then I found my blankets.

***

It took us another week to reach OKC. We had gathered more cattle and done a small amount of trade on the way in. Our herd numbered over two hundred head, mostly young stock. When we reached OKC, we sold off the older stock, putting the herd to roughly one hundred thirty.

We camped outside the wall, holding the herd there until we resupplied the wagon. Shep and two of his dogs rode in and placed our resupply order. We'd schedule it to be picked up in two days. Coder, the other two dogs, and I stayed at the wagon and kept watch over the herd.

"When Shep gets back, we'll go check in at the PK office. They usually have someone on duty here. We'll update our pads, and you can have a look at the server room."

Coder nodded, "I bet there will be a lot of repair work there."

"You are probably right. We'll take a look, and then decide if we need to stay longer to let you catch up the repairs. No word from Captain Vance?"

He shook his head, "Nothing."

I nodded and felt riders coming in. I could see two men riding easy toward us. They felt relaxed, but I stayed alert all the same. They rode straight to our camp and reined up.

"Good morning," one said.

"Morning. Step down and have a cup of coffee," I said.

"Thank you."

They climbed down and ground hitched their horses. I handed them a cup and poured the coffee.

"Name's Buford, John Buford, and this is Jim Bozeman, one of my hands."

I nodded. "I'm Price, and that's Coder," I answered.

Nice looking herd. Would you be interested in selling some of them?"

I nodded, "How many you thinking?"

Buford squinted, one-eye thinking. "'Bout twenty-five or thirty. I want to add some young stuff to my herd. This would be easier than brush poppin' 'em."

"By a long shot," Bozeman said, smiling.

I smiled, "True. You go through and pick out the ones you want. We'll settle up after you look them over."

"That'd be fine. Y'all come up Forty-Four?"

I nodded, "Yep."

"How was the trail? They been having a lot of trouble down the Thirty-Five. Marauders have been raiding southeast."

"Trail was good. No trouble that we heard about all the way to OKC," I said.

"Good to hear. Well, we'll get to it then. They turned their cups upside down on the ground at the fire and stepped to their horses.

"I'll ride over in a bit, and we'll see what you have," I said. Buford nodded, and they moved off to the herd.

I gave them time to look over the herd, and then went out to them. They had decided on twenty-five. We settled on a price, and they started moving them on. I concentrated on a few of them and told them to follow their new herd. I was not as good at it as Shep was, but the cattle moved on without any trouble.

Shep was back by lunch, so Coder and I went into the PK office. No one was there, but they had left a message. The message was three days old. Three PKs had gone south down Thirty-Five to investigate the troubles there. There was also a message for any scouts that passed through to activate and follow.

"Well, so much for our plans to leave tomorrow," I said.

"There is some work for me here. It will keep me busy for a few days anyway," Coder said.

I nodded. "You catch up on the work here, and then you and Shep can move on to Tulsa. I'll either meet you on the trail or in Tulsa. I need to go back to the wagon for some gear. I'll tell Shep what's going on."

"Step lightly, Scout."

"You too."

I stopped at the trading post and picked up trail supplies, hard rations, and ammo. I charged it to OKC and the PK. Then I rode out to the wagon, where Shep was cooking dinner.

"Trouble?" he asked.

"Some, I've been activated by the PK. I'm headed south to help find the marauders down Thirty-Five."

"I heard there was trouble while I was ordering supplies. Prices are up a bit."

"Coder has some work to do at the PK office. Go ahead and buy all the supplies we need. Y'all can head for Tulsa when he's finished his work, and I'll either meet you on the trail or in Tulsa."

Shep nodded, "We'll see you then. Step lightly, Scout."

"You, too, brother."

I packed the gear I needed for the trail, which wasn't much. I was travelling light. I did strap my AR-10 case to Talon; it might come in handy on this trip. Shep made me a meal of bread and meat that I ate as I rode.

We stopped the first night in Moore, and the people there said the PK had passed through three days ago but had no other information. I grabbed a quick bite and moved on out of town and made a cold dry camp.

We made it to Norman the next night. I put Talon in the stable and fed her well. No use in rushing into anything. I had a hot meal and a bed for the night.

I showed my badge to the bartender. "PKs come through here a few days ago?"

He nodded. "They were headed south. There's been trouble between here and Paul's Valley."

"What kind of trouble?"

"Supply wagons taken, cattle stolen. So far as I've heard, they've only been hitting travelers on the Thirty-Five."

I nodded, "Thanks." I finished my beer and went to bed.

After eating an early breakfast, Talon and I were on the road again. We started riding parallel to the Thirty-Five, watching for trouble. When we'd see travelers, we'd ask about the conditions south. So far, all said it was quiet. I guess with PKs in the area, things had calmed down.

CHAPTER 8

We were not rushing to catch up with the other PKs. I didn't want to jump into anything I'd need to rush away from with my tail on fire. I'd stop for dinner, make a small fire, and have hot food and coffee. Then I would put out the fire and move on a mile or so to cold camp for the night. Weather was holding, so it wasn't too bad.

I'd unsaddle Talon at night for her to roll and forage as she wanted. She always stayed close to me. Between the two of us, nothing was going to take us by surprise.

We came up on a trail where a lot of horses had passed heading northeast. The PKs had followed the new trail, and so did we. They were all moving fast, so we picked up our pace. There must have been fifteen or twenty horses in the lead group. They had apparently realized that the PKs were on their trail, as they were only stopping long enough to rest the horses. Then they were off again.

I'd walk beside Talon while we rested, but we kept moving. We were closing on the PKs. I don't think we were more than a day behind them. We seemed to be headed toward Shawnee, or that general direction anyway.

We needed a rest, so we stopped, ate a hot meal, and I had coffee. We moved on, and then camped. Talon rolled a bit, but she stayed in camp. I lay there, resting and looking at the stars.

"Oh, I'm an idiot."

I sat up, took out my data-pad, and opened the map screen. Sure enough, the three PKs were marked on the map, as was I. They were about ten miles ahead of me, still headed toward Shawnee. Looking at the map, with all our locations marked, made me nervous. I didn't like the idea that someone knew where I was. I turned my locator off. I'd plead ignorance if asked about it. I slept better after that.

We were on the trail before sunup. I wanted to catch up with the PKs today if possible. No one was trying to hide their trail; they were just running. That made me cautious.

I found the PKs camp midafternoon and found them an hour later. They had ridden head long into an ambush. The marauders had stopped running and waited for them.

The PKs lay where they fell. Everything of value had been taken: guns, gear, and horses. I took the PKs' fingerprints to ID them, and then we buried them. We ate an early dinner. Then, we were back on the marauders' trail.

They were riding hard. I assumed to put some distance between them and the ambush site. Smart move. No matter, I'd find them eventually. I had not known the PKs, but they were PKs. I'd collect the debt owed for them.

I was now hunting. Talon felt my change in mood and did likewise. I got a message from Coder; they were now on the trail toward Tulsa. That was one less thing for me to worry about.

Talon and I started moving more at night and rested during the day. Moving was slower, but with Talon's better night sight, we moved at a good walking pace. We no longer made a fire, so it was cold camps until this was over.

***

We had been moving all night, so just before sunrise, we stopped for the day. I unsaddled Talon. She rolled and then lay there and slept. She had an odd habit of sleeping. Sometimes she slept like a horse standing. Other times, like now, she lay down. I leaned my back against a tree, ate some hard tack, and closed my eyes while I chewed. I decided I would far rather be working my wagon trade business than this.

Suddenly, the tree bark beside my head exploded, cutting my neck, head, and face. I rolled into the bushes, and then behind the tree.

Talon jumped up and ran into the woods, but not too far away. I could feel her anxiety, so I let her know I was okay. The shot had to have come from a good distance away. The only mind I felt was Talon's.

Work your way toward the east. That is where the shot came from. Don't get too close. When you feel his mind, stop and let me know. I felt Talon's mental nod, as she moved away.

I stayed on my belly and backed away, staying behind the tree I had been leaning against. I kept moving back, putting more trees between us. I was sure the shooter was moving by now, or at least he should be. I pulled my scout cape out of my daypack and put it on. In retrospect, I should have been wearing it.
I stayed low and slow moving south.

Found him. Talon sent. *Stay there, but keep away and out of sight. He'll probably be moving.*

I moved to where Talon was, and when I was almost to her, I felt the other's mind. He must have already moved his position, as he was still now.
I went further, circling around behind him. I took my time. Now was not the time to rush. I must admit; I did enjoy the stalk. I could see him and felt no others around. I moved closer, until I felt I was close enough. Then, I mentally punched him in his temple. He slumped, out cold. I eased forward, making sure he was out, and he was. I called Talon to me.

I got rope from my bags and tied his hands behind him. After tying his feet together, I tied them up to his hands. Then I emptied his pockets. He had a few dollars, a pocketknife, pistol, belt, and shells. It was a decent rifle, though, a bolt action .30-06.

Find his horse and bring it in. Talon moved away.
In a short time, she returned. *Found his camp. His horse is here but not saddled.*
Okay, come back. We'll move to his camp.

When Talon got back, I loaded the shooter over her saddle, and we moved to his camp. He had a basic camp, decent horse and saddle. I sat him against a tree and put some water on to boil. I cleaned my wounds while waiting for him to come to.

I took his picture and printed him. Greg Doorman was his name. He was wanted for cattle rustling, and now attempted murder of a PK.

I looked through his gear and found a coffee pot and coffee. It had been days since I'd had any, and I was ready for some. I put the pot on to boil.

My wounds weren't deep but had bled a good bit. Scalp and face wounds usually did. I felt him starting to wake up, so I poured myself a cup of coffee and waited. He opened his eyes, looking around to get his bearings.

He focused on me, and then shook his head. "That's life ain't it? One moment you're looking down the barrel on a target, and the next you're tied up waiting for the hangman."

I shrugged. "It's a hard business we're in."

"That's the truth of it. I don't know how I missed you. I had you dead on."

"You didn't miss by much. One inch would have seen me off."

"Well, they say a miss is as good as a mile."

I poured him a cup of coffee and sat it down beside him. I cut his hands free and stepped back.

"Obliged," he said.

I sat back down by the fire. "You in on the PK's ambush."

"Naw, I was scouting ahead when that happened. After that, they left me here to watch our back trail. I was to leave today if no one showed," he said, sipping his coffee.

"Your group the ones raiding up and down the Thirty-Five?"

He looked at me and then at his coffee. He shrugged, coming to a decision. "Yeah, I mostly scouted for them. We took mostly supply wagons and cattle herds. Usually left regular folks alone."

"Twenty men is quite a gang, don't usually see that many together."

He nodded. "A new man in the area hired us on in ones and twos. He goes by Aka Smith, as in, 'Also Known As' Smith. He thought it was really funny," he said, smiling.

"You set the ambush sight? It was a good one."

"No, we knew they were coming. Smith tracked them on a data-pad he has."

"So, he knew I was coming too."

"Yeah, but he lost you somehow. That's why he left me."

I nodded. "Any last requests?"

"Yeah, decent burial and another cup of coffee."

I nodded and picked up the coffee pot. When he held out his cup, I shot him dead.

"Sorry, only enough left for one," I said, pouring my cup full. I did give him a proper burial though.

***

I sent a message to Coder: "We were being tracked through a stolen PK data-pad. At least one ambush has been carried out, killing the three PKs. Turn all the location trackers off. Email Twisted Knee an update. I'm still on the trail."

"Done," he messaged back.

Talon and I continued to travel at night. I still had nineteen men to find, so I continued following them. They bypassed Shawnee to the east and continued north. They weren't travelling as fast, but they weren't lettin' moss grow on 'em either.

Two nights later: *I smell smoke on the wind, not strong, so not close,* Talon sent.

Follow the scent, and let's see what we find. They may have coffee, I answered, smiling.

It took us an hour's time to find the camp, and there were four men in the group. I got close enough to listen and waited.

"How long we going to wait?" one asked.

"Smith said two days, so we wait two days. Unless you want to leave early and tell him you got tired of waiting," the leader answered.

"No, I was just wondering," the others chuckled.

That was all I needed to hear. I waited for them to bed down for the night. One stayed up on guard, and the others were just about asleep. I concentrated, and one by one I crushed the brain stems of the sleeping men. With that done, I finished the guard by crushing his brain stem as well.

We moved into camp, and I unsaddled Talon. I took their pictures and printed them for ID. I poured myself a cup of coffee and began searching through their gear. Anything I could not use or sell I tossed to the side, which wasn't much. You could sell most anything at a trading post.

I took the gear and the horses with me when we left the next morning. I left the dead men where they lay. They weren't worth the effort to bury.

***

I sold the horses and gear at the next trading post I came to. They asked no questions, and I offered no explanations beyond that I was a PK Scout. I bought a few things and was on their trail once again.

North of the Forty Trail, they split into two groups. One headed east toward Okmulgee, and the other continued north toward the Forty-Four Trail. I followed the bunch heading north. That was toward where Shep and Coder would be. At our next stop, I messaged Coder that a group of marauders was heading their direction and to be vigilant. We started travelling day and night now. I wanted to catch up with this bunch quickly.

I continued north, following the marauders. From their tracks, there seemed to be seven or eight. We were moving by day again. I saw no need to push harder. Talon and I were already covering more ground than they were. We were back to our normal travel routine—hard tack breakfast and lunch on the more. After a hot dinner and coffee, we were on the move again before stopping for the night.

Talon and I didn't speak much, but I felt the presence of her mind with me. It was like being in a room with someone you were comfortable with and didn't feel the need to talk to enjoy each other's company. We camped just before dark. I wanted to be on the trail early, so I went straight to sleep.

***

°You'll be leaving soon?° Mandy signed.

°Yes, as soon as I turn fifteen.° I signed.

She was looking at her feet in the creek water. I sat beside her, watching her from the corner of my eye. I got my nerve up; it was now or never.

"Mandy," I said. She looked at me. "If you are agreeable," I swallowed a lump in my throat. Her eyebrows raised. "You're almost fifteen, too, and I'd like to ask your mother if we could be married."

She made a sound I had never heard her make before. It was like a large cat's yowl. She launched herself onto me, wrapping her arms around me and holding me tight. I lay still, but she wouldn't let go. I knew she was okay because she was making her content cat's purring sound. I waited with my arms around her.

She finally sat up. Her face was tear streaked, but she was smiling. °Yes, ask your grandfather to speak to my mother. She will say yes. I will make you a good wife. I will keep our home and give you sons.° She stopped and frowned. °What of my mother? She has no one but me.°

I nodded, taking her hands. "She will be part of our family until she takes another mate. Until that time, if ever, she will live with us."

Her smile split her face, and with tears streaming, she buried her head into my shoulder. We lay on the bank of the creek. Her gentle purring made me smile.

"Come on," I said, "let's go talk to the old man."

Mandy sat up. °No, you must do that alone, and then he must come to see Mother.°

"Okay." I stood up, looking serious. "I do have one concern." She cocked her head at me, frowning. "What dowry will you bring me?" Her face went blank, and she growled. I ran, laughing. She let out a scream like a puma and caught me in less than four strides. Her tackle put us both in the creek. She sank one of her claws into my butt cheek. "Ow, that's cheating!" I yelled, laughing. Further dowry negotiations were put on hold until I was out of the reach of her claws.

We walked home, holding hands. I left her at her porch and went to find the old man. He and mom were sitting at the kitchen table having coffee. I poured myself a cup and sat down with them. They were both watching me. I usually didn't drink coffee except at breakfast, so they knew I wanted to talk.

"I would like you to go to speak to Mandy's mother for me," I said, looking at the old man.

He frowned. "About what?"

Mom slapped him on the arm. "Stop it. You know good and well what."

"All right, I'll go see her next week," he said. Mom just stared at him. "Okay, okay, I'll go see if she's home."

Mom shook her head. "And where else would she be?"

"You never know," he said over his shoulder as he walked out the back door.

Mom started dinner, while we waited for the old man to get back. "I'm guessing you and Mandy have talked about this?" Mom said.

"We did," I answered.

"Did she ask about her mother?"

"She did. I told her I wasn't marrying her mother," I said, smiling.

Mom didn't even turn around. "You are too much like you grandfather sometimes."

I chuckled. "Her mother will be part of my family for as long as she likes, or until she takes another mate."

Mom nodded. "Good, that's good," I heard her sniff.

I knew she was crying. She and Mandy's mom had been friends since childhood. Mom had been hoping I would take her in but had never mentioned it.

I heard the old man walk up on the porch. He came in and took his seat at the table.

"Don't start any trouble," Mom warned.

He chuckled, nodding. "It's settled. You and Mandy are to be married when you return from your proving journey. Mandy said the two of you had decided to take her mother as part of your family." I nodded. "Good," he said. "That is a fine thing you've done, and it put both of their minds at ease. I'm proud of you."

That was the first time he had ever said that, and I felt my chest swell a little.

***

We were on the trail before sunrise, and I sure missed my morning coffee. The trail was still easy to follow, as they were making no attempt to hide it. I still didn't take any chances though. One near miss on this trip was enough.

A concussion of an explosion broke the morning quiet, followed by gunfire. I leaned over Talon's neck, and she plunged into the brush and headed straight for the sound of battle. Another concussion sounded as we started up the side of a ridge. When we topped the ridge, I could see the firefight below. As I feared, it was Shep and Coder's camp.

I jumped from the saddle and opened the AR-10 case. Pulling the weapon out, I seated the mag holding the armor piercing rounds. I dropped to the ground and unfolded the bipod legs. From a small rise, Shep's M-60 crashed their party and started calling a new tune. That sent the attackers scrambling for cover.

I didn't take time for anything fancy. AP rounds center mass would get the job done. I sighted my scope on their rear-most man. At this range, there wasn't much of a ballistic drop. Shep was keeping them busy. I squeezed off my first round, and the impact of the 7.62 knocked him flat. A man rose, aiming an RPG. I fired as quickly as my crosshairs passed over him.

The round took him in the hip, but he still fired the RPG. It impacted off target, but the M-60 went silent. I didn't have time to worry about them now, I moved on to the next target. The men below heard my next shot, they now knew someone else had joined the party. As one would make a break for the horses, I'd put him down.

"You boys had enough?" I shouted down.

"You're a PK, so you'll hang us anyway. You're going to have to come down and get us," one shouted back.

My crosshairs were already on him. I shot him through the neck, almost taking his head off.

"Have it your way," I shouted.

They fired a few shots at where they thought I was. None came close. I changed to non-AP rounds. I wanted to save them. It took me a little while to whittle them down. I'd shoot an exposed foot here, and an exposed arm there, causing them to make a run for it. In the end, they all died. It was a hard line of work they were in.

I moved off the ridge and toward where I thought Shep and Coder were. I found them in a shallow depression. They were bloody and battered, but alive. I checked to make sure they were bandaged well enough.

"I'll go check to make sure they are all dead," I said.

"Let the dogs do it," Shep replied.

Only two dogs responded to Shep's call. The others had been killed. They found one barely alive, but he wasn't for long. Seems dogs hold grudges too.

I hung the dead men with a sign that read, "Marauders and PK Killers."

We dug through the wreckage, put together a meal, and had coffee. "What a mess," Coder said. "Both wagons are a total loss, stock dead or shattered."

"Don't worry about it. I can replace wagons. People can't be replaced. We'll rebuild and carry on." Shep's dogs were at his knees, and he was quiet. "Shep, I'm sorry for your loss."

He nodded. "They were good hounds."

I nodded. "Yes they were. The best I'd ever worked with."

We sat in silence the rest of the evening.

CHAPTER 9

The smell of smoke, explosions, and gunfire still hung in the morning air. I was up early and started the coffee. Shep's two dogs lay beside him but watched me moving around the camp. I sat down beside the fire, waiting for the coffee to boil. Coder was right. This was a mess, but at least we were still here to clean it up.

Both wagons were a total loss, along with a lot of what they carried. We'd stay here a few days and lick our wounds. My mind kept turning to the other group of marauders and Aka Smith. I still had unfinished business with him. My biggest concern was whether he would come to find out what bad happened to his men or just cut his losses. To assume either option put our lives in danger.

The smell of coffee got Coder and Shep out of their blankets. I filled their cups, and we sat in silence, enjoying our coffee for a few moments. Both of them where looking around at what was left of the camp. A few cattle had wondered back in.

Coder poured our second cup. "Plans?" he asked to no one in particular.

"Well," I started, "the wagons are a loss, but we can cobble something together. The wheels look okay. We'd probably be better served going to the closest town to buy a new wagon or two. Someone would stay here to guard the camp. We'll salvage what we can and go to Tulsa."

"We'd need at least two," Shep said.

"We have another problem," I added. "The group that attacked yesterday was not all of the gang. I was trailing them, but they split in two. I followed this one, fearing they were heading toward y'all. Now, I'm wondering what the other group will do. They might cut their losses and run, or they might come here to find out what happened to their friends."

"Sapulpa is the next town on the way to Tulsa," Shep said. "If we can't get wagons there, we'll try again in Tulsa."

"And the marauders?" I asked, already knowing the answer.

"You have to go find them," Shep said. "Coder can go for the wagons, and the dogs and I will stay here until he returns. We'll scavenge what we can, and you can meet us in Tulsa when you finish your business."

I nodded. It was the only plan that made sense.

"I'll leave after I eat. Take your time, and don't risk yourselves. We can buy replacement supplies." They nodded.

***

I found the marauders four days later. They were on a ranch southeast of Okmulgee. I spent the day watching and circling the ranch. I didn't want any surprises. There were thirteen men, two women, and two children. The women were younger but looked hard used. The children didn't look much better. I was not going to waste time with this bunch, but I did want to talk to Mr. Smith.

Smith stayed in the main house with the women and children. Most of the men slept in the bunkhouse. There was also a barn where two other men slept. The last light went out at about ten o'clock, but there were roving guards moving around the place. I lay down and slept for a few hours, letting the guards get bored.

I woke around two and felt where everyone was. All were asleep, except two out on roving guard. The two in the barn were asleep, so that seemed a good place to start. I moved down behind the barn and went in through a side door. Both men were out cold in the loft. I concentrated on them and crushed their brain stems. It took more mental strength to crush their brain stems than to put someone to sleep. I was already getting a killer headache from using my talent so much, and it was also taking more of an effort to sense minds.

I left out the side door, circling around to the bunkhouse.

One of the roving guards was at the far end of the yard, the other at the main house. I didn't need to go into the bunkhouse, as I could feel each of the eight minds. I moved down the wall of the bunkhouse, putting each man into a deeper sleep. Doing that was easier and took less effort.

The outside guard continued his rounds. I moved to the front door of the bunkhouse and went inside. The men inside were in a deep sleep. I took a seat and waited. Before long, the guard from the main house came out and headed for the bunkhouse. He was coming to wake the next guard shift. Taking a piece of stove wood, I moved behind the door and waited. He entered, closing the door behind him. I hit him in his head, not really caring if I killed him. He dropped right where he stood.

I put him in a chair at the card table and lay his head down on it like he was sleeping. It didn't take long for the roving guard to get antsy, and he came looking for his replacement. I broke the store wood over his head, laying him out in the floor. I picked him up and put him on a bunk. Then, I put the two unconscious men into a deeper steep. Gathering rope, I tied everyone up.

Everyone in the main house was still asleep. I moved around to the bedroom windows. Concentrating, I put everyone into a deeper sleep. Once I was sure they were out, I went inside. Once inside, I lit a lantern and started coffee and breakfast for myself. I was tired, and my headache was much worse, but I'd just have to deal with it. I still had work to do. I ate my breakfast and had a couple cups of coffee. I rested for a while, letting my headache ease off.

I went into the bedroom where I assumed Smith was asleep with one of the women. The other bedroom was for the children and other woman. I decided to wake the woman sleeping with the children. I moved her into the kitchen, tied her to the chair, and gagged her. I sat down across the table from her and made sure my PK badge was in plain sight. Then, I woke her.

She was slow to stir, but I was in no rush. I had another cup of coffee. Her head finally came up and her eyes focused. She realized she was tied. Her eyes became large with fear, focused on me, and then on my badge. She looked around the room and back at me.

"Are you fully awake?" I asked. She nodded slowly. "My name is PK Scout Sargent Price. The children are safe and asleep, as is the other woman." Hearing that, she seemed to calm down. "The man with her, his name is Smith, right?" She nodded. I got up and un-gagged her. "What's your name?" I asked.

"Marcy," she answered.

"And the other woman?"

"Jenna, my sister."

"The children?"

She shrugged. "They were here when we arrived two years ago. The men took us as slaves." She didn't say anymore, and she didn't need to.

"You don't have to worry about them anymore. I've taken care of them, and I'll be taking care of Smith shortly," I said.

"Hanging is too good for him," she replied.

"You are probably right. He'll have to answer to God for his sins. I'll just arrange their meeting. You got family?"

She shook her head, eyes tearing up. "They were killed when we were taken."

I untied her. "Let's get your sister up."

We got Jenna from the bedroom and woke her up. Marcy kept her calm and explained what was happening. They held each other and cried, and I just let them cry it out.

I went to the room where Smith slept and tied him up. I searched the room. If he had money, he would keep it close. In my experience, greedy people always did. I found a strong box in the chest at the foot of the bed. The key was in Smith's clothes that were piled in the corner.

I unlocked the strong box. There must have been fifty or sixty thousand dollars inside. That seemed like a lot of money for a bunch of raiding cattle thieves. A data-pad was also there. I closed the box, relocked it, and went back into the kitchen. The ladies were more composed, as they sat watching me. I poured myself another cup of coffee and sat down.

"I'll be taking Smith down to the bunkhouse to talk to him.

You get the children up and make breakfast. Stay in the house. You don't need to worry about what's going on outside."

"You going to hang them?" Jenna asked.

"They are marauders, rapists, murderers, and thieves. They also killed three Peacekeepers, so they are under an automatic death sentence. I may not actually hang them, but they won't see another sunrise."

"Good," was all she said.

They got up, started breakfast, and began to wake the children. I picked Smith up and moved to the bunkhouse. I tied him to a chair beside the other man. I looked around at the men, considering what I would do. I needed answers, but these were hard men. No matter, they would find no mercy in me, but dying in their sleep was a mercy. I started a fire in the potbellied stove and put coffee on. Then I went to the barn and got branding irons.

I stoked the stove, good and hot, and put the irons in. After waking everyone up, I poured my coffee and waited. They were madder than a bag of cats and screamed and fought against their ropes. Those at the table turned the chairs over trying to break free, and I drank my coffee, waiting. I noticed one of the men did not wake up. He was gone, I had put him under too deep, and he was brain dead. I guess we might as well get this show started.

"My name is PK Scout Sargent Price. You are all guilty of killing three PK officers, which is a death sentence. Let me be clear; you are going to die. How hard you die is up to you. I need information. Those who give it to me will leave this world quick and easy. Those who don't will stay longer and beg me for a final death. Now, some of you think you are some hard men. You think PKs are not as hard as you. Maybe. But I'm a PK Scout."

I put my coffee cup down and took my nano-bladed knife out as I walked to the brain-dead man's bed. The blade passed easily through his neck, removing his head. I sat the severed head on the table. "So let's get started, shall we?"

That brought on more screaming and fighting. I waited, drinking my coffee and checking the heat of the branding irons. Once they had quieted, I cut the laces on one man's boots, and pulled them off his bare feet.

"I read an old history book that Roman soldiers who were caught sleeping on duty, and for other minor infractions, would have the soles of their feet beaten with a cane. They said the nerve endings stop in your feet, making the pain twice as intensive. It also left the rest of your body undamaged so they could go back to duty sooner. It said very few men fell asleep on guard duty twice." I took an iron out of the stove and moved back to the barefooted man.

"I don't know nothing," he shouted, fighting his ropes.

"I haven't asked anything yet," I said. "Who gives you your orders?" I moved the hot iron close to his feet.

"Smith, we get all our orders from Smith. He tells us what to do."

"Who gives Smith his orders?"

"I don't know. He gets messages from the data-pad he has. Then he tells us where to go and what to do."

I nodded. Like a snake striking, I stabbed him in his heart. He died quickly. I looked around. "As promised, a quick death," and I put the iron back in the fire.

"He's a killer right enough, but boys, I don't think he's got the stomach for the work." I looked around at the man talking. "We ain't seen him do nothing but kill one man. I say spit in his eye, and don't tell him nothing. Go out with some backbone."

I took another iron from the fire and walked slowly over to "mouthy's" bunk and stared at him for a moment. Smiling at him, I pushed the white-hot iron into his crotch, setting his pants on fire. I held the iron in place as he screamed. When he passed out, I pulled it back. His pants were still smoldering, and the smell of burnt flesh filled the room.

"Save your spit; you're going to need it," I said, putting the iron back in the fire. "Shall we continue?"

***

The rest wanted and got a clean death, but I kept "mouthy" alive as a reminder. The severed head was still on the table, staring at Smith and the house guard.

"You must be Smith's second in command," I said. He said nothing. "Who wants to go first?" I said, smiling. "First question, where did a bunch of low lifes like you get over 50,000 dollars?"

They looked at each other, saying nothing. I could feel the number-two guy getting nervous, though he hid it well. I reached over and ripped open Smith's shirt, laying his chest bare. I took the branding iron from the fire and pressed it to his chest. He screamed and passed out. I held the iron in place, letting it cook for a moment, as I glared at number two.

I put the iron back in the fire and took a drink of water. "This is thirsty work," I said. "What's your name?" I asked number two.

He licked his lips. "Kennedy, Ray Kennedy."

"So, Ray, how and where did you get over 50,000 dollars? There ain't that many cattle to be stolen, and there ain't been no banks robbed."

He looked at Smith's blistering, burnt chest, "Payroll for thirty men, plus bonuses."

"Paid by who?"

"Don't know his name; he's just called 'The Gentleman'. He sends us messages on the data-pad for jobs he wants done, and then sends us payroll to keep this many men on full-time."

"Where does he operate out of?"

"Smith said Orleans, never been there myself."

"How do you get the payroll?"

"Courier, or a message to meet some place. If it's a meeting, Smith always goes."

"So, what was the latest job?"

"We were to raid south of OKC and Tulsa to draw out PKs. We were to kill every one we could.

"Anyone specific?" I asked, walking behind him.

"All PKs in general, but we'd get a bonus if we got a PK Captain named Vance."

I stabbed him up through the back of his head, killing him instantly. I put Smith into a deeper sleep and went back up to the main house. I went in the back door and into the kitchen. The two ladies and the children just stared at me.

"We'll be staying here another day. Go ahead and take care of the livestock, and do your chores like you normally would. Stay out of the hay loft though." They all nodded and went about their daily work.

I got the data-pad from the strongbox and went back to the bunkhouse. I used Smith's fingerprint to open the data-pad, and then changed the lock to mine. I started looking through the files and pictures on the data-pad. Smith struck me as the type of man who would want an ace up his sleeve.

I found a few pictures of the same man. All the pictures were taken in hotels, and he was always nicely dressed, like a gentleman. I woke Smith up and had the data-pad sitting in front of him.

"Tell me about The Gentleman," I said.

Smith looked over at Kennedy. "Well, now that it's just you and me, let's make a deal," he said.

I smiled, "I made you my offer."

He nodded. "You did, and you've kept it. I'd like to make a counteroffer." I said nothing. "I'll tell you all I know about The Gentleman and his operation, if you give me your word I leave here alive with half the money. And you'll never hear from or about me again."

"How about I cut you to pieces and figure it out myself."

"You could do that, but why waste the time? I'm nothing to you, and no one will miss the money. I've already done all the work for you."

I looked hard at him. "Five thousand and a horse."

"Twenty-thousand."

"Ten thousand, or I start carving you up."

He nodded. "Ten thousand and a horse."

"If I feel the information ain't worth ten thousand, you'll go out hard."

He nodded. "His name is Dean McCormick, and that's his picture. He's from back east, from old family money. He came to Orleans and bought a casino and hotel. He lives in the hotel. He fancies himself big, wants to build a dynasty. He's been pushing out smaller operators in Orleans over the past few years, and now he's moving west. He wants to become, what he called, a Cattle Barron."

"What's he got against PKs?"

"He wants to be the law in his kingdom, and PKs will get in his way."

"What's he got against this PK Captain Vance?"

"Now that I don't know. From the little I do know, being around him, it seems personal. Maybe Vance got in the way of a business deal or something. He never said."

"Are you the only gang he was running?"

"No, he's got people all over. He works mostly East Texas, Louisiana, South Arkansas, and Eastern Oklahoma. He also runs boats up and down the Mississippi."

"Ambitious man."

"He is and, with his casinos and other operations, he's well funded."

"That seems strange to me, all this just to own cattle. With all that money he could buy several ranches."

"I asked the same thing. He smiled and told me not to think too much. I never asked again."

"Do you know any of the other gangs on the frontier?"

He shook his head. "No, he kept everyone separate, never used names, and never spoke of other operations. I found out some of this from the courier who brought in the payroll. I got him drinking, and he liked to brag."

"Anything else?"

"Yeah, you don't cross him but once. That's why I'm heading west and will disappear. I don't want you or him looking for me."

"You do that."

I left him tied to the chair and went back to the house and put the data-pad back into the strong box. Then I took out ten thousand dollars, walked to the barn, and picked out the worst horse there. After putting the worst saddle on him, I returned to the bunkhouse.

I tossed the money on the table. "As agreed, ten thousand.

There is a horse outside." I cut his ropes. He took the money and left as fast as that nag would carry him, never looking back.

The ladies were sitting at the table when I went back to the house. "Why don't you make a big meal? You can use whatever you want from the supplies. You all look like you could use a good meal."

They smiled. "That's a fact," Jenna said.

I went back outside and started gathering all the gear worth taking. We'd take all we could when we left. They were good cooks, which was probably why they were still alive. They made fried pork chops, beans, corn, bread, and sliced tomatoes. There was plenty of it, and they ate like it may not come again.

"Mr. Price?" I looked at Marcy. "What's to become of us?"

"We'll leave here tomorrow and head for City-Fort Tulsa. You ladies are of an age to decide what you want to do for yourselves."

Before I could say more, Jenna said, "We'll keep the children."

I looked at the children and saw fear in their eyes. "Fine by me. That's y'all's business. As far as I know, you are all kin." They relaxed at once. "I know people in Tulsa; we'll get you set up."

"Where will we stay?" the boy asked.

"In your own house. There's money to set you up and take care of you."

He nodded and went back to eating.

***

We didn't leave the next day, as it took a while to load the wagons. There was a lot of salvage to load. We left the following morning in a four-wagon train. Talon kept all the horses with us, and we made good time on the trail. We sold off some of the salvage as we passed trading posts and towns. We also bought new clothes for the four. They weren't quite in rags, but they didn't miss by much.

Our wagon train pulled into the Tulsa wagon station mid-afternoon on the seventh day of our trip. Shep and Coder were already there.

"Looks like you've been busy," Coder said.

"Some," I answered. "We'll talk later." He nodded.

The wagons were put in the barn and the horses in the stock-yard. Shep and Coder had brought in three wagons, the Morgan oxen, and some horses. They didn't bother with the cattle.

Nora took to the children and the young ladies like long lost kin. She put them up in their house for now; we were all tired. After dinner, Shep, Coder, and I sat at a fire and shared coffee.

"How was the trip?" I asked.

"Could have been worse, bought wagons at that small town and salvaged as much as we could. Had to move slow because of the Morgans," Shep answered.

"It looks like you were successful," Coder said.

I nodded, taking a swallow of coffee. "Yeah, I found what was left of their gang," I said.

I gave them the story of what had happened at the ranch, but left out the part about making a deal with Smith. I'd tell Coder about McCormick later. I trusted Shep, but that was PK business.

"So, Smith had a PK data-pad and was tracking us?" Coder asked.

"Yep, that's why I had you turn off all tracking. I got it back so you can look it over in the morning. Maybe you can figure out where he got it. I need to file a report and email Captain Vance, but we'll take care of all that tomorrow."

***

Coder and I went to the PK office after breakfast. There was no one at the office, but we still went into the back tronics repair room to talk. I told him what Smith had told me and showed him the pictures of McCormick.

I filed a partial report, saying all the marauders had been killed. I sent an email with pictures of McCormick to Captain Vance, telling him he had an enemy who was gunning for him and who it was. We left the tracking option off. Someone else might be using it against us. Coder looked at the data-pad Smith had been using. It had not been an active PK pad for a few years.

Later that afternoon, I took Nora, as my accountant, to the bank. We opened accounts for the two ladies and the two children. I put ten thousand dollars into each account. That would see them educated and start them out in their new lives. Nora would help them manage the accounts.

We bought them a house close to the wagon station and got them set up. I used the rest of the money to replace the loss of my wagon and supplies. Ben had one of his wagons completed and was working on another. I bought the completed wagon but was not sure if I'd buy the second. If I did, I'd have to wait for it to be finished.

We were looking over the new wagon, and Coder made the tronic upgrades.

"You still thinking about taking a herd home?" Shep asked.

"Yeah, I'm just not sure whether I should wait for the second wagon to be finished or go on ahead with only the one."

"Well, if you decide to wait, I'd like a new wagon," Coder said. "Not as big as yours, but bigger than the normal ones. I want one built for tronic repair with room for me to sleep in."

"We can do that. That actually sounds like a good idea. You and Ben talk over what you want. We'll have him get started on it as soon as he finishes the other one."

We pitched in helping with the wagon's build. It helped pass the time, and we were finished faster. We put in a cupola to Coder's wagon and added a machine gun when we were able to. We had kept the RPG tubes from the attack. Now, we just needed to find the rockets for them.

We stayed in City-Fort Tulsa for two months, finishing our wagons, but they were finally done. We sold or traded off all of our salvage and divided the spoils. Then we moved all of Coder's tronic parts into his new wagon and loaded the trading wagons with supplies.

We left early morning, headed east for a day, and then turned southeast. We stayed off the major trails. There would be more mavericks on the less-travelled routes. It felt good to get back out on the trail. The city walls felt like they were closing in.

Shep drove the first supply wagon, and Coder drove the second. The horses pulling Coder's tronics wagon followed behind without a driver. As usual, Talon and I scouted ahead.

We fell back into our trail routine, working well with each other. Game was plentiful, and I took fresh meat every few days. Gathering mavericks started slow, but the farther we got away from Tulsa, the more we picked up. We didn't do much business for the same reason. Most made the trip to Tulsa every month or so to resupply.

We travelled north of Fort Smith through the old Ozark National Park. The weather was good, for the most part, and travelling was easy. We were doing more trading now and got a cow for a few pigs. They trooped right along behind the wagons. We stayed well north of Conway, turning north to Heber Springs.

We sat around the fire, having coffee. Shep, as usual, was singing to the herd. Our herd consisted of cattle, horses, pigs, sheep, and goats. I feared Shep would trade for chickens, ducks, and geese next.

Shep poured another cup of coffee. "Sugarloaf?" he asked.

I nodded, "Yeah."

"We have dessert?" Coder asked.

Shep chuckled, "Not tonight."

"Sugarloaf Mountain," I said. "That's where we are headed. Well, that area anyway, Heber Springs area."

"I'd have rather had dessert," Coder said, smiling.

"Maybe tomorrow," Shep said.

"They know we are coming?" Coder asked.

"They do; they've been scouting us for a few days," I answered. "They'll meet us when we turn toward the Sugarloaf in a day or two."

I found my blankets and stared at the stars. I was thinking of Mandy as I drifted off to sleep.

CHAPTER 10

We sat on the porch and watched the sunset. Mandy turned toward me. °How long do you think you'll be gone?° she signed.

°I don't know. I have to prove I can survive out in the world. I have to prove I can make my own way and provide for my family. I cannot fail, and I cannot come back with nothing.° I answered.

°I know, but I care nothing for things. I care for you.°

°I know that, but I must prove myself to the elders. It's our way.°

°Stupid way.°

I smiled. °Maybe. I'll be back as soon as I can, and then we'll marry.°

She nodded, putting her face into my chest.

***

It was two days before we turned in toward the Sugarloaf. We stopped the herd in an open area beside a river.

"We'll stop the herd here, as we'll have company later," I said.

Our herd numbered over three hundred head of cattle, most of them

young. We had kept some old stock to keep them all settled.

We set up camp, and Shep made a large pot of meat stew, some freshly baked bread, and apple pie. Just before sundown, three riders approached. They came in the open, plainly seen. I stepped away from the fire to greet them and recognized one of them right away. It was Chuck, the first guy I had knocked out when he tripped Mandy.

"Greeting, brothers," I said in Clannish. "Come to our fire and be welcome."

"Thank you, brother," the eldest said. They stepped down

from their horses and followed me back to the fire.

"We were about to eat. Will you join us?" I asked.

"Yes, thank you."

Shep served up the plates, and we all sat and began to eat.

"How was the trail to Fort Smith?" Elder asked.

That was their version of small talk while we ate. Shep served pie and coffee, as talk turned more serious.

"You have done well for yourself, Price. You will not need to recount your deeds before the Counsel. We have all heard of PK Scout Sargent Price. The herd you bring gives more credence of your good fortune, as do your wagons." I said nothing, letting them speak. "You have returned to claim your bride?"

"I have, I have proven my worth and have returned."

Eldest looked at Coder and Shep. "May we speak plainly?"

"Yes, I trust these men with my life."

He looked at Chuck and nodded.

I felt Chuck's anxiety level rise.

"Mandy's mother asked me to speak to you." I raised my eyebrows. "She did not wish you to be surprised. Perhaps blindsided would be a better word."

"About?" I asked.

"When we were children, we made fun of Mandy about having some cat traits and her being a mute. Well, before you showed me the error of my ways," he said, smiling. "Anyway, her appearance has changed since you have been gone. She has taken on more aspects of a cat."

"In what way?"

"Her eye color and teeth, and now she has fur covering her body. Because of this, some have shunned her."

I felt my temper starting to rise. "Have any mistreated her?"

"No," he said, shaking his head. "No, they have not, but Mandy has withdrawn. Her mother thinks Mandy fears how you will react to her, seeing her changed appearance."

I nodded, thinking. "Thank you for telling me this, but it changes nothing. I have come for my bride. However, I understand how she may feel." I looked at Eldest. "With your permission, I'd like to go see her and put her mind at ease. I'm sure she already knows I have returned."

"She does, and you may. Present yourself to the Counsel at noon in two days." I nodded, walked out to Talon, mounted, and rode out.

***

I rode up into Mandy's yard shortly after full dark. A lantern lit the front porch. Mandy's mom stepped out of the house.

"Greetings, Mother," I said, as I would do a mother-in-law.

"Greetings, Son," she answered. "You have talked to Charles?"

"I have."

She nodded, "Step down."

I dismounted, moved to the foot of the stairs, and waited. I could feel Mandy inside. I felt her fear. She came out onto the porch in a cloak, with the hood up hiding her face. She stopped at the top of the stairs.

°I will hide nothing from you.° she signed.

Her mother moved behind her, and they removed the cloak. Mandy stood before me in her two-piece bathing suit, her head hanging. She had grown into a woman.

Her facial features had changed little. Her ears were a little more prominent, sticking out of her shoulder-length hair. The biggest change was that most of her body was now covered in a fine golden-spotted fur. It reminded me of a cheetah's coloration from pictures I had seen.

"I'm sorry," I started. A yowl of anguish started from Mandy. "Stop," I said. She did, looking up at me through green cat eyes with black slitted pupils. "I'm sorry it took me so long to get back to you, but I have returned to claim my bride. As far as I'm concerned, nothing has changed."

°Our children may turn out to look like me.° she signed.

"I hope so," I said, smiling. "You are far better looking than I. And no matter what they look like, they will be loved. Your appearance changes nothing. If anything, you are more beautiful than I remember."

She leapt off the porch into my arms, squeezing me tight.

Her mother was laughing and crying at the same time. "I told you he was in love with you, not your looks." Mandy looked at her, nodding. "Now go inside and get some clothes on."

Mandy nodded and started up the stairs. That's when I saw she had a short tail, like a lynx or bobcat. Before I thought, "You have a tail," I called. She yowled, put a hand over her tail, and ran inside. I laughed, "I love all of you," I shouted.

"We have missed you so much and are so glad you are back," her mother said.

"I've missed you too. My mother is well?"

"She is, and she has taken a new mate. He is kind and good to her. She lives with him now, so your house is empty. I have also met someone, but was waiting for you to return before accepting his offer."

"I am happy for you," I said.

"Thank you. You need to talk to Mandy before you make any further plans. Things have changed for her here."

"Chuck told me some of it."

"People can be mean and superstitious. I don't think Mandy wants to stay here. She may want you to take her away."

"We'll talk, and I'll do whatever makes her happy. May I stay in your barn tonight?"

"Of course."

Mandy came back out, wearing a nice dress. She seemed to have changed. The set of her shoulders was different. She was no longer afraid, and that made her all the more beautiful.

°I'm glad to see you, my love, but you need a bath.° Her mother put her hand over her mouth, stifling a laugh.

I dropped to my knees, "But I have returned to claim you. Ride away with me this night. Right now, I say," I said in my most dramatic voice.

°I'm not going anywhere with you until you bathe. When you are clean, we'll talk. We also have pie and coffee, and there is a towel and soap laid out for you in the bathroom.°

"I have to bathe before pie? That don't hardly seem right."

Mandy put her hands on her hips. I recognized the look. "Let me take care of Talon, and then I'll be in." She nodded and went inside with her mother. I walked Talon to the barn.

I like her. She will be a wonderful mate, Talon sent.

Yes, she will.

***

We sat at the kitchen table, enjoying the pie and coffee. "They say you have brought a herd of cattle in with you," Mandy's mom said.

"I did, three hundred cattle, along with pigs, goats, sheep, and any other critters Shep could call up or trade for."

I told them how we operated and gathered mavericks as we travelled and traded. I also talked bout how his dogs worked the stock and watched over them and the camp.

°What will you do with them all?° Mandy signed.

"That depends. What do you want to do? We could start a ranch with them, here or elsewhere, or we can sell them off and go somewhere else."

Mandy leaned forward, taking my hands. "I do not want to stay here. Take me away, so we can start new somewhere else," she said.

I was shocked. Her voice was a soft purring whisper. I sat with my mouth open looking at her.

She looked at me, smiling. "Another change," she said in her whispering voice.

"Then we shall sell the herd and go elsewhere. We own a wagon station in Tulsa; we'll start there. We have enough money and can live anywhere you'd like. We can start a ranch anywhere. You tell me, and I'll make it happen."

She was smiling with tears in her eyes. "Thank you," she whispered.

I smiled. "So, you have your wedding dress?" She nodded. "How much room will you need in the wagon for your things once we leave?"

"Not much. I only have my hope chest," she whispered.

"Wedding plans?" I asked.

Mandy looked at her mother. "It will be a small affair, just family," her mom said.

"Is that because of the way people have treated Mandy?" There must have been an edge to my voice, as Mandy lay her hand on mine. "Sorry, you know how I feel about bullies." She nodded. "Well, a small wedding will not work for me. We will be having a feast. I will provide the meat, and everyone else will provide the rest. People will know by now I have brought in a large herd and two huge wagons of supplies. They will want some of both, and I want you at my side when they come to ask about buying. You won't have to say a word. I'll know by the way they act who mistreated you."

"You have a mean streak," her mother said, smiling.

"Only when someone hurts my family, and both of you have been family for years. I won't do anything crazy. I just want to let them see what it feels like to be looked down upon. Now, about the dowry."

Mandy growled, and I jumped up and ran out the back door, laughing the whole time. I looked back, but no one was chasing me. I heard her mother laughing.

"Mandy said to tell you, you have to come back sooner or later. So you might as well get it over with," her mother shouted from inside the house.

I stepped to the back door. "In my defense, she didn't let me finish. What I meant to say was I brought her bride price."

Mandy came to the door. "Choose your next words carefully. If you say you have brought a goat, pig, or chicken, you will regret it."

"Don't be ridiculous," I said. "We don't have any chickens."

Among the other changes Mandy had gone through, her speed was one of them. She leapt on my back, as I left the back porch, and rode me to the ground. I was laughing so hard I couldn't catch my breath.

Mandy's mother was sitting on the back steps, laughing. "I'm sorry, dear, I didn't catch that last part."

"I said I have brought Mandy's bride price."

"That part I heard. It's what came next that I missed," she said, smiling.

"Well, Mandy mentioned chickens, and I said I didn't have any."

"I see. Then what do you offer for my beautiful daughter?"

"Two hundred head of cattle," I said. Mandy sat up, looking at her mother.

Her mother was taken aback for a moment, and then smiled. "Your offer is a little low, but I see my daughter has feelings for you. So we accept."

***

It was early, but I had been up for a while. Mandy came into the barn. "Come to breakfast," she said, holding out her hand. I took it and walked up to the house.

Breakfast was already on the table, so we sat down. "Plans for today?" Mandy asked.

"I need to go to the trading post to see Junker. I don't want to undercut his business, so I need to resupply him first. I'll see what he says before I do anything. Would you like to go with me?"

"I would," she said, smiling.

After we finished breakfast, I went back to the barn and saddled Talon. Mandy was ready when I walked Talon up to the house. She was dressed as I remembered her: pants, a blouse, vest, and boots. She no longer hid under a cloak.

Mandy stepped down from the porch. "She is beautiful."

"This is my good friend, Talon. Talon, this is my soon to be wife, Mandy."

I am most pleased to meet you, Mandy, Talon sent.

Mandy's eyes got big, and her hand went to her mouth. "You heard that?" I asked, frowning.

She nodded. "I did. How wondrous," she said, smiling.

Mandy concentrated. *I am most pleased to meet you as well,* Mandy sent.

Now it was my turn to be shocked, as I had heard Mandy. "My

goodness."

Mandy looked at me. "You heard?" she whispered. I nodded. "More changes, I guess."

"That is amazing," I stopped. "Let's keep this between us."

She nodded, *Okay.*

We mounted Talon and rode to the trading post. We were greeted along the way. We dismounted at the trading post and went inside.

"Good Morning, Junker," I said.

"Good Morning, Price. Welcome back."

"Thank you. I've come to talk to you about resupplying you from my wagons. I don't want to undercut your business, so I came to you first."

He cocked his head at me. "That is kind of you."

"Just good business. I'm looking at starting a supply run out this way, and I'd want you as a customer."

He smiled. "Good. What can you offer me?"

"It will save time if you ride out to our camp and see for yourself."

"I can do that," he answered.

We rode out to our camp, and I made introductions. "Gentlemen, may I introduce my bride to be, Mandy." They stood, removing their hats. "Mandy, this is Coder."

"Pleased to meet you, ma'am. Now I see why Price brought us all the way across the country. I would have too."

°Thank you,° she signed.

"And this is Shep," I said.

°I am very pleased to meet you,° he signed.

Mandy smiled. °And you as well, Shep,° she signed.

"You are just full of surprises, aren't you?" I said to Shep.

"What can I say, I'm a deep individual," he answered. We all laughed.

"This is Junker; he owns the trading post. Shep, see what kind of deal we can come to. Just keep us enough supplies for the trip into Conway. We'll resupply there."

"You'd be better served to go into Little Rock and resupply

there. You could make a resupply sale to stores in Conway. The money you'd make would be worth the difference," Junker said.

"We'll talk about it," I answered.

We left Junker with Shep and rode out to look over the herd.

I've never seen so many in one place, Mandy sent.

You wait until you see Shep sing to them at night. I've never seen the like.

*Do you want to start a ranch somewhere? *

Maybe, but that's not my be-all, end-all dream. We have a wagon station and the beginning of a trade route. I'm thinking we should concentrate on that for a while. We'll go back to Tulsa and see if you like it. We can do both, have a ranch somewhere and have wagon stations for trading hubs. Mainly, I just want to be where you are.

I felt the vibrations of her purr of contentment on my back and smiled.

***

When I announced we would be having a wedding feast, and I would provide the meat, the community was all for it. Anyone else just needed to bring the other foods. Mandy's wedding dress was nice, but she made it even more beautiful on. After the wedding ceremony, as expected, people approached to ask about buying supplies or cattle. Mandy had calmed me down, so I just pointed everyone to Junker and her mother for supplies.

Mandy's mother was a shrewd trader. I ended up letting her sell off the rest of our herd, including the goats, pigs, and all. It saved us work. Overall, it was an enjoyable day, and everyone was on their best behavior.

Mandy's mother stayed in town so we could have the house to ourselves on our wedding night. We got back to Mandy's house about midnight and didn't come out until the next afternoon. If I had known what was waiting for me, I would have come back sooner.

Coder was sitting out at the barn. That was unusual, so I got dressed and went out to speak to him. "Everything okay?" I asked.

He handed me a data-pad. "Email from Vance."

I took the data-pad. It read, "I need you and your friend to activate, meet me in Tulsa, and I'll brief you then. Message me when you are a week out."

"What do you think it's about?" Coder asked.

"If I had to guess, McCormick or some of his dirt. You and Shep unload the supply wagons at the trading post. We'll leave in the morning." He nodded and left.

I sent the captain an email: "In route. See you in a month."

I went back inside. Mandy had coffee ready. "Anything wrong?" she whispered.

"My PK Captain has activated Coder and me. We need to meet him in Tulsa. We'll be leaving in the morning."

She looked at me. "Who are you including in that *we*?"

I chuckled. She held up a finger. "Don't start none, won't be none."

"What?" I said, laughing. She gave me the look again. "Okay, you are included in the *we*."

"Smart man."

We packed what Mandy wanted into her hope chest; we'd pick it up later. We rode into town to see her mother and to say goodbye.

"So soon?" her mother asked.

"I'm sorry, but the PK has activated me. I have to go."

"I understand," she said, hugging us. "Write when you get settled."

"We will," Mandy said.

We unloaded the supply wagons at the trading post. Junker had bought everything we wanted to sell. We then loaded the remaining supplies into one wagon, giving Mandy and myself the other for our home on the road.

Mandy and I stayed at the camp with Shep and Coder. We'd leave at sunup in the morning. Shep made dinner with dessert. Then, as we sat around the fire, Shep played his guitar and sang. The dogs took right to Mandy, cat or not.

I was at peace and relaxed for the first time in a long time. My eyes were getting heavy. Looking past the fire into the night,

I thought I saw the old man. He stood at the edge of the fire light, smiling...then he was gone.

OTHER BOOKS BY JAMES HADDOCK

The Derelict Duty

Prologue:

The Blaring klaxon jolted me out of a sound sleep. I threw my covers off and was halfway to my Vac-suit locker before I was fully awake. It felt like I had just fallen to sleep having just finished a long EVA shift. It would be just like Dad to have an emergency drill after an EVA shift to see if I had recharged my suit. I had, I always did, both Mom and Dad were hard taskmasters when it came to ship, and personal safety. Vac-suit recharging was top of the personal safety list. If you can't breathe, you die, easy to remember.

Donning a Vac-suit was second nature for me, after 16 years of drills and practice exercises. Having literally been doing this all my life, but I loved life on our Rock-Tug. I was reaching for the comms when I felt the ship shutter. "That can't be good," I said to myself.

Mom's voice came over ship-wide, "This is not a drill, this is not a drill, meteor strike, hull breach in Engineering". Mom's voice was just as calm as if she was asking, what's for lunch. This was a way of life for us, we trained and practiced so that when the reality of working in "The Belt" happened you didn't panic, you just did your job. You didn't have to think, you knew what you needed to do, and you did it.

I keyed my comms, "Roger, hull breach in Engineering, where do you need me Mom?" "Get to Engineering and help your Father, I'm on the Bridge trying to get us in the shadow of a bigger rock for some protection." Mom answered. My adrenalin was spiking but Mom's calm voice, helped to keep me calm.

I sealed my helmet and left my cabin heading for Engineering. The klaxon had faded into the background, my breathing was louder than it was. I kept telling myself "Stay calm, just do your job, stay calm."

I had just reached Engineering, when the Tug was rocked by a succession of impacts each one harder than the last. The hatch to Engineering was closed and the indicator light was flashing red, telling me there was hard vacuum on the other side. I switched my comms to voice activated, "Dad? I'm at the hatch to Engineering it's in lockdown, I can't override it from here." "Dad? Dad?, Dad respond!

"Mom, Dad is not answering, and Engineering is sealed, you are going to have to evac the air from the rest of the ship, so I can open the hatch." Mom's steady voice replied, "Understood, emergency air evac in 10 seconds."

Those were the longest 10 seconds of my short life. The hatch indicator light finally turned green and the hatch door opened. The Engineering compartment was clear. No smoke, no fire, some sparks and lots of blinking red lights. I looked over to the Engineering station console, there sat Dad. He had not had his Vac-suit on when the hull was breached.

Hard Vacuum does terrible things to the human body. I suddenly realized that I had not heard Dad on comms the whole time, just Mom. She probably knew what had happened but was sending help in the hope that Dad was all right and that maybe the comms were down.

I heard Mom in the background declaring an emergency and calling on the radio for help. Her voice still calm somehow, "Mayday, mayday, this is the Rock Tug Taurus, Mayday, we have taken multiple meteor strikes, have multiple hull breaches, please respond."

"Come on Nic, think! What do I need to do?" I asked myself. I closed the hatch to Engineering, to seal the vacuum from the rest of the ship. I turned and started back toward the bridge. There was an impact, a light flared, and sparks; time seemed to slow, there was no sound, we were still in a vacuum, just shuttering vibrations and sparks. Holes seemed to appear in the overhead and then the deck, it was so surreal.

The meteors were punching holes through our ship like a machine punching holes on an assembly line. "Meteor storm"

Duty Calls

Duty Calls continues the story of Nic, Mal, Jazz and Jade as they fight to hold what belongs to them. The Corporations are becoming more aggressive in their effort to steal their inventions. Our four friends are matching the corporate's aggression blow for blow. The fight has already turned deadly, and the Corporation has shown they aren't afraid to spill blood. Nic has shown restraint, but the gloves are about to come off. They've gone after his family and that's the one thing he will not tolerate.

From Mist and Steam

Searching the battlefield after a major battle Sgt. Eli finds a dead Union Army messenger. In the messenger's bag is a message saying the South had surrendered, the war was over. Along with the Union Messenger was a dead Union Captain carrying his discharge papers, and eight thousand dollars.

Sgt. Eli decides now is a good time to seek other opportunities, away from the stink of war. While buying supplies from his friend the quartermaster, he is advised to go to St. Louis. Those opportunities may lie there and a crowd to get lost in. Sgt. Eli, becomes Capt. Myers, a discharged Union Cavalry Officer, and strikes out for St. Louis.

The war has caused hard times and there are those who will kill you for the shirt you are wearing. Capt. Myers plans on keeping his shirt, and four years of hard fighting has given him the tools to do so. Realizing he must look the part of a well-to-do gentleman, he buys gentleman clothes, and acts the part. People ask fewer questions of a gentleman.

What he isn't prepared for is meeting an intelligent Lady, Miss Abigale Campbell. Her Father has died, leaving the family owned shipping business, with generation steam-powered riverboats. They have dreams of building steam-powered airships, but because she is a woman, there are those who stand against them. Capt. Myers' fighting is not over, it seems business is war. They decide to become partners, and with his warfighting experience, and her brains the world is not as intimidating as it once seemed.

Hand Made Mage

Ghost, a young Criminal Guild thief, is ordered to rob an ancient crypt of a long dead Duke. He is caught grave robbing by an undead insane Mage with a twisted sense of humor. The Mage burns a set of rune engraved rings into Ghost's hand, and fingers. Unknown to Ghost these rings allow him to manipulate the four elements.

Returning to the Guild to report his failure, everyone thinks he has riches from the crypt, and they want it. While being held captive by the Criminal Guild, Ghost meets Prince Kade, the fourth son of the King, who has troubles of his own. Ghost uses his newfound powers to escape from the Guild saving the Prince in the process.

Spies from a foreign kingdom are trying to kill Prince Kade, and Ghost must keep them both alive, while helping Prince Kade raise an army to stop an invasion. Ghost finds out trust to soon given, is unwise and dangerous. He is learning people will do anything for gold and power. As Ghost's power grows, his enemies learn he is a far more deadly enemy than anything they have ever faced.

Mage Throne Prophecy

A routine physical shows Captain Ross Mitchell has a flesh-eating virus that specifically targets the brain. Prognosis says he'll be a vegetable by week's end. Having survived numerous incursions in combat around the world, Ross decides he's not going out like that. He drives a rented corvette into a cliff face at over 200 MPH. The fiery impact catapults him toward the afterlife.

Instead of finding the afterlife, he finds himself in a different body with an old man stabbing him in his chest. He fights free, killing the old man before passing out. He wakes to find he's now in the body of Prince Aaron, the 15-year-old second son of the King. In this medieval world, the Royals are Mages. The old man who was trying to kill him was a Mage "Vampire". Instead of blood, the old Mage was trying to steal Ross/Aaron's power, knowledge, and in this case, his body. When Ross/Aaron killed the old Mage, his vampire power was transferred to him.

He now has the memories, knowledge, and powers of the old Mage. Ross/Aaron must navigate this new environment of court intrigue with care. His older brother, the Crown Prince, hates him. His older sister has no use for him. The King sees him as an asset to be used, agreeing to marry him to a neighboring Kingdom for an alliance. Before the marriage takes place, the castle is attacked.

Someone is trying to kill him but is finding it most difficult. Where Mages fight with Magic, Ross/Aaron fights with magic and steel. It's hard to cast a spell with a knife through your skull or your throat cut. As Ross/Aaron travels with his fiancée toward her home for the marriage to take place, they are attacked at every turn. Someone doesn't want this wedding to happen. Ross/Aaron has had enough of people trying to kill him. With Aaron's knowledge, and Ross' training, they take the offensive. The Kingdom will never be the same.

Wizard's Alley

Scraps, a gutter child, is sitting in his hiding place in a back alley, waiting for the cold thunderstorm to pass. Suddenly, lightning strikes in front of him, and then a second time. The two lightning bolts become men—two wizards—one from the Red Order, the other from the Blue.

The Red Wizard, chanting his curses, throws lightning bolts and fireballs. The Blue Wizard, singing his spells, throws lightning bolts and ice shards. So intense is their fighting, they become lightning rods. It seemed as if God Himself cast His lightning bolt, striking the ground between them and consuming both wizards in its white blaze. Scraps watched as the lightning bolt gouged its way across the alley, striking him.

Rain on his face awakens Scraps. The only thing left of the fighting wizards is a smoking crater and their scattered artifacts. He feels compelled to gather their possessions and hide them and himself. The dispersed items glowed red or blue, and he notices that he now has a magenta aura. Magenta, a combination of both red and blue, but more powerful than either.

Scraps then does what he has done all his life to survive. He hides. And unknowingly, he has become the catalyst for change in the Kingdom.

Cast Down World

In the summer of 2257, the asteroid Wormwood was closing in to strike Earth a glancing blow. Even a glancing blow would be catastrophic. Earth's governments and militaries united to try to shift Wormwood's path. Earth launched every nuclear missile she had and succeeded in changing its path, just enough to miss her surface. In doing so, shards from the asteroid, caused by the nuclear blasts, struck the earth. In those shards were spores that caused a change in all forms of life. Wormwood also changed Earth's magnetic field, affecting weather patterns and causing earthquakes and tidal waves.

The devastation caused society's collapse. Only the strongest survived the Great Dying. In the years that followed, mutations began to appear in animals and people. It was a time of lawlessness, where the only law was the one you could enforce. Cities and larger towns became walled city-forts. Some chose to live outside the city-forts as ranchers, farmers, and scavengers. They enforced the law with violence, and the law of the old west returned. Out of this came the Peacekeepers, modeled after the legendary Texas Rangers. They were empowered by the city-forts to be judge, jury, and executioner. They were a group of hard men: hated, feared, and respected.

This is the story of Price—a human mutation, raised in the frontier wilderness—who becomes a PK Scout.

Printed in Great Britain
by Amazon